HER MAIL ORDER MISTAKE

LONDON JAMES

D1736910

long
VALLEY
PRESS

ONE

LILY

*L*ily closed her bible and held it against her chest, whispering the verse back to herself, "May the God of hope fill you with all joy and peace as you trust in him, so that you may overflow with hope by the power of the Holy Spirit."

It was a verse she knew well. A verse she had read so many times while growing up that it was so etched into her brain, she doubted she could forget, even if she tried.

She inhaled a deep breath, letting it out as she closed her eyes.

The door to the bedroom opened with a force that slammed it into the wall behind it. The sound made her jump, and she nearly fell off the side of her bed.

"Give it back to me, Patrick," Suzy shouted.

"You want it? Come and get it." The boy, nearly two feet taller than his younger sister, jumped on the bed nearest him and waved the girl's small teddy bear in the air. He made a mocking laugh before jumping off the other side of the bed and darting to the other end of the room.

"I said, give it back." The little girl's voice cracked, and her eyes brimmed with tears.

Her brother laughed and teased her with the stuffed toy once more before running out of the room.

"Miss Whittaker is going to have your head," Lily called after them. Whether the six- and eight-year-old heard her, she didn't know. But as she heard Miss Whittaker's voice at the end of the hallway, she knew little Patrick had been caught. It was the lecture Lily had heard, she didn't know how many times in the last ten years in the orphanage. One hundred. Two hundred. Five hundred. She didn't know. There were always little boys running around, taking things from the little girls. Whether it was their sister, it didn't matter. They would do it to just any little girl. They didn't care. Occasionally, it would be two girls fighting over something, whether it was a hairbrush or a pretty hair comb they both wanted to wear that day.

"And I better not catch you stealing your sister's toy again," Miss Whittaker said as she entered the bedroom. She stopped in the door frame, pointing down the hallway. "Patrick? Did you hear what I said?"

"Yes, ma'am," a little voice called back.

She let out a huffed breath as she came into the bedroom. "And how are you today, Lily?" she asked.

"All right, I guess."

"Did you finish with all your morning chores?"

"Yes, ma'am."

"And when was the last time you bathed?"

"The other day, ma'am."

The older woman smiled. "Well, do it again before you leave."

"Leave?" Lily's brow furrowed, and her heartbeat kicked up a notch. "Where am I going? Do you need me to run to town for a few things?"

"Oh, no. I did all my shopping a few days ago." Miss Whittaker smiled again, then moved around the side of the bed and sat on the end. Her movement caused the mattress to shift a bit under Lily. "I have news, dear, and I don't know how you will feel about it."

"Is it bad news? Are the other Headmistresses going to make me leave because I'm no longer a child?"

Miss Whittaker's face scrunched and Lily, thinking she might get sick, hurried off the bed and over to the window. She grabbed the drapes, gripping them so tight that her skin turned pale from a lack of blood.

"They are going to make me leave, aren't they?"

"Well, yes, and no. I have spoken to them, and I think I have bought you some time. But this is an orphanage for children, Lily, and you are not a child anymore. You are a grown woman."

"But I have no place to go, and I have no money."

"Aren't you always talking about traveling to find your father? Maybe you could do that?"

"I have no money. I have a name and town he lives in. That's all. I do not know if he is still alive or if he knows about me or would want me to find him."

Miss Whittaker rose off the bed and made her way over to Lily by the window. Although it wasn't cold outside, Lily trembled, and the older woman reached for her hands, cradling them.

"I have spoken to the other Headmistresses, and they all agree that you can stay for a little while longer. But it's only a little while, and they have told me I need to find you another option, which is why I'm here. Another possibility has come about, and I wanted to see what you thought of it."

"Thought of what?"

"I received a letter today from a man who is a marriage broker in Montana."

"A marriage broker?" Lily's stomach twisted with her words.

She didn't know what it was, and she also didn't know if she wanted to know. "What is a marriage broker?"

"Well, dear, it's a man who takes advertisements from other men who are . . . well, who are looking for a wife."

"Are you suggesting that I become the wife of a man I've never met?" Lily took a few steps away from the older woman. Her heartbeat kicked up even faster at the thought. She had never even talked to a boy outside of the ones who came into the orphanage, and they were always younger than her and had other things on their minds. And now she was supposed to just marry one?

"I don't think I can do that." She brushed her fingers against her neck before clutching it. Miss Whittaker lunged forward, grabbing Lily by the shoulders.

"I know what I'm asking of you. But I wouldn't ask it if I didn't have to. They won't give you much time to stay here, and I don't want you to get turned out into the street."

Lily thought of all the times she went on errands for Miss Whittaker or one of the other Headmistresses, and she would see the homeless people walking the streets. They wore nothing but tattered clothing and were often rooting around the alleys looking for any scraps of food they could find. Most of them talked to themselves, leaving people passing by alone, but there were times when they would shout at people or wave their hands, acting as though they could attack at any moment. Miss Whittaker often told Lily they behaved that way because their hard lives had driven them into a state of madness.

She didn't want to go mad.

She also didn't want to live without a roof over her head or dig for scraps of food.

Rubbing her hand across her forehead, she fought back her tears. "So, what would I have to do? Am I supposed to write this man?"

"No, dear. He wrote to me asking if I knew of a lovely young lady who would be interested in marrying the son of a wealthy sawmill owner." Miss Whittaker gave Lily a half-smile. "It's the chance for a good life. He said that the young man is a fine young man and him and his family will care for you. It seems like a rare opportunity, and I think you should take it."

Lily glanced around the bedroom. The only place she'd known for the last ten years. While there were pictured images from the house she shared with her mother, they were such distant memories that she wondered if they were real or imagined. She always knew that one day she would have to leave this place. The problem was, she had been hoping that day wouldn't come.

"He's a nice young man?" she asked Miss Whittaker.

"That's what the letter says. And he's from a wealthy family. This could be an amazing chance for you."

"If he's so nice and wealthy, though, why does he need a man to find him a wife?"

"I don't know, dear. Perhaps he is busy, or perhaps too many other women are after him and he doesn't know how to pick."

Lily knew the older woman was grasping at any excuse to make her feel better. But the truth of it was that she didn't feel better. There were far too many questions for her to ask, and she knew that no matter how many times she made any inquiry, it didn't matter. No one would give her the answers she sought.

"Well, all right then. I suppose I will meet this young man."

"I will let Mr. Benson know."

"Mr. Benson? Is that the father?"

"No, dear, Mr. Benson is the marriage broker. Mr. Townsend is the father of the young man. Zachary Townsend of ... Lone Hollow."

"I beg your pardon. Did you say Lone Hollow?"

"Yes, dear. I guess it's some tiny town close to Butte. But not close either. I can't say that I've ever heard of it myself, but that was what was in his letter. Do you know the town?"

Lily backed away from Miss Whittaker and made her way back over to the bed. She knelt on the floor and reached under the bed for a small box that was wedged in the corner between the bed frame and a small bedside table—two things allowed for each child who slept in this bedroom of the orphanage.

"Isn't that the box your mother left with you when she left you here?" Miss Whittaker asked, looking at the rusted pieces of tin.

Lily nodded as she opened the top and peered at all the trinkets inside. A necklace her mother gave her as well as a feather from a bird's nest she'd found when she was ten or eleven. Plus, a thimble that Miss Whittaker had given her, along with a small sewing kit and a scrap of paper with her mother's handwriting etched across it.

"What is that?" Miss Whittaker asked.

"It's my father's name and the town he lives in. My birth father. My mother gave it to me just before she left me here that day."

Miss Whittaker outstretched her hand and took the piece of paper as Lily handed it to her. She read the name and town and her eyes grew wide. "But it says Lone Hollow. That means you'll be in the town where your father lives?"

"If he still lives there. He could have moved on or even died."

"Well, I think it's still fortuitous, and you never know what will happen." The woman smiled and handed Lily the scrap of paper back. "I shall go down to my office and write him at once. And then tomorrow, we will take you into the dress shop across town and buy you some new dresses." Lily opened her mouth, but Miss Whittaker waved her hand to stop her. "Oh, don't worry. We won't get you anything too fancy or spend a lot of money. But I do have some saved up, and, well, I'd much rather spend it getting you a few smart dresses than keep it wrapped up in a handkerchief in my dresser drawer. Consider it a wedding present." She reached up, cradling Lily's cheek in her hand. "I remember when your mother bought you to the orphanage. You were just nine, and you had these big blue eyes —the biggest I'd ever seen in a little girl. I can't believe that was all those years ago. And look at you now. You're going to be a married woman soon."

Married.

What a thought.

While Lily had always imagined herself married and having a family of her own, she couldn't deny there were other dreams in the back of her mind. Dreams of becoming a doctor, and even though she knew it would never come to pass, she never could bring herself to let go of the hope.

One day there will be women doctors, she would think to herself. *One day.*

Lily opened her mouth, but as she did, there was a huge crash downstairs, and someone started screaming as though they were dying.

Miss Whittaker and Lily rushed down the stairs and into the kitchen, where Suzy lay on the floor, rolling around and screaming in pain. Her skin was bright red and burned, and a steaming pot lay on the floor beside her. Miss Whittaker rushed for her.

"What happened?" she asked the little girl.

Suzy pointed to the stove and then to the pot. Tears streamed down her face. Her arms and legs were getting redder by the second, and her skin looked like it was blistering and starting to peel.

"What is happening?" Lily asked Mrs. Whittaker.

"She burned herself with the boiling water. I put the pot on before I came up to talk to you. I forgot about it."

"It's all right. It's not your fault." Lily turned toward the hallway where Patrick stood, pressed against the wall. His eyes were wide, and his mouth gaped open. "Patrick, go fetch Doctor Hamilton." The boy shook his head. "Yes, you must. I can't, and

Miss Whittaker can't. We can't leave your sister. Now, go. You know where his home is. He's just down the lane. Go!"

"What do we do for her?" Miss Whittaker asked.

After watching the boy dart from the house, slamming the door behind him, Lily stared at the girl for a moment. She'd read something somewhere in one of the medical journals she'd come across in her studies. Just because she couldn't attend school—proper school—didn't mean she didn't keep up with her medical interests.

"Hold on. Let me think."

Think. Such an impossible thing when a girl was screaming bloody murder feet from her.

"Wasn't there an article you read? You made me get those supplies to have in the house just in case of burns."

Yes. Burns. What were those supplies? And where was that article?

"Get some cold compresses on her while I try to find the article I read." Lily dashed up the stairs and back to the bedroom, flipping through the pages of the stack of books on her bedside table. By the time she found it and made her way back downstairs, Miss Whittaker had covered the girl with wet rags. The girl screamed louder every time the material touched her skin.

"Do we have any wool?" Lily asked.

"There is a blanket in the hallway closet."

"Get it and cut it into strips. And where is the linseed oil?"

"In the cabinet." Miss Whittaker pointed to the cabinet in the back of the kitchen as she darted toward the hallway.

Lily rushed to the cabinet, searching through the bottles until she found the linseed oil. "And do you have the lime-water liniment?" she asked the headmistress as she came back into the kitchen.

"It should be in there too."

Lily turned back to the cabinet, finding the second bottle.

"Alright, we need to apply these and cover them with the wool strips. It should help the pain and fight off infection until the doctor arrives."

The two women worked, applying the oils, and laying the strips over the girl's arms and legs. She screamed for several more minutes, but after they lay the last strip on her arm, she calmed as she lay on the floor. Her body trembled from shock, and she sniffed as tears still streamed down her cheeks. Lily sat beside her, both watching the girl and trying to read the article in case there was something she'd missed.

Sweat beaded along her forehead, and although she tried to wipe it from her face, it clung to her skin. She closed her eyes and counted. It was the only thing she could think to do to pass the time until the doctor arrived to help her remain calm.

By the time Doctor Hamilton rushed through the front door and made his way into the kitchen, the girl had begun to wiggle from pain again. Lily took off several bandages, pouring more of the linseed and lime-water liniment mixture on the burns and applying new strips. The doctor watched her for a moment but then took to checking the girl's vitals—her pulse, her eyes, and listening to her heart.

"We need to get her to my office," he said.

"Is she going to be all right?" Miss Whittaker clutched her throat as he stood and faced her.

"If we can keep the burns from getting infected, she should recover." He glanced over his shoulder down at Lily. "If it weren't for her quick thinking with the oils and bandages, I would have been too late. That young woman saved the girl's life."

TWO

RODERICK

"*I* just can't marry you."

Emily's words repeated in Roderick's mind. Although he wanted to forget they were ever uttered—and especially from the lips of the woman he loved—he couldn't shake them. Like one of those blasted songs that got stuck in his head, they washed through him. Again. And again. And again.

He stood at the window of his bedroom, looking down on the front yard of his parent's home. He'd thought nothing of the grass or bushes for as long as he could remember. They were just there—nothing to consider. But now, they were all he wanted to think about. A foolish thought to him, and yet one he clung to. For if he didn't think of the foliage, his mind would drift back to the night Emily ended their courtship a little over two months ago.

He didn't want to pretend he didn't know why she'd done what she did. It was obvious. It was because of the accident. And it was because of the scar that now ran down his face, from his hairline down to his chin. The deep wound that had healed but left its mark—a permanent reminder of what he almost lost that day at the sawmill.

It'd been one of those days. Something in the air had felt off. But he'd ignored it, and now he was paying the price.

A knock rapped on his bedroom door, and he turned toward it. "Come in."

The door popped open, and his mother strode in. "Good morning, my son."

"Morning, mother."

"And how are you feeling?"

He cast her a glare before turning his gaze back to the window. "How do you think I feel?"

"There's no need to take that tone with me, young man. I wasn't the one who ended your courtship."

He opened his mouth to respond but closed it and took a deep breath instead. His mother was right. It wasn't her fault. She didn't leave him. Emily did.

"My apologies, Mother."

"Did Emily say anything else before she left? Is she going to write to you from Butte?"

He shook his head. "No, and I doubt she will."

"Well, what reasons did she give? You didn't tell me the entire conversation and your father, and I have been left to wonder what all was said."

"There's no reason to tell you everything. None of it matters except she told me she couldn't marry me."

"But did she say why?"

"She said she no longer could love me. That her parents have certain expectations for their family, and I no longer fit those expectations."

"I don't understand."

He spun and pointed to the scar running down his face as he raised his voice into a growled shout. "It's because of this!"

His mother stepped back and laid her hand on her chest for a moment. She blinked a few times and then shook her head as though to shake off her son's anger. "There is no need to shout at me. I didn't do this to you."

He closed his eyes, inhaling and exhaling a few more breaths to calm himself. "I know you didn't, Mother. My apologies again for my outburst."

She brushed the sides of her dress and folded her arms across her chest. "Well, I think she's a fool, and I think after some time in Butte, she will realize it too and come crawling back."

He snorted. "And what I am supposed to do then? Take her back? After she's realized that there is no one else, I'm supposed to be the second choice over a spinster's life?"

"That's not what I meant."

"I know, Mother. And I shouldn't have suggested that is what you meant. It's over and done with. Emily is in Butte, and I am in Lone Hollow. Our courtship is no longer, and you should cancel any wedding plans you had already made." He turned to face her. "Was there a reason you came up here?"

"Your father wishes to speak to you."

"Oh, goodie. That is just what I need this morning."

Another growl rumbled in Roderick's chest as he strode past his mother, out of his bedroom, and down the stairs to his father's office. So few words had been spoken between the father and son in the last several months with the accident, and then the ended relationship between the Townsend and the Sanderson families. He didn't have any idea what could be on his father's mind this morning. Gut instinct told him; however, he probably would not like this conversation either.

He knocked on his father's office door, and after his father told him to come in, he entered the office, shutting the door behind him.

"Mother says you wish to see me," he said.

"Yes. Come. Sit. I have a few things to discuss with you."

His stomach twisted as he sat in a chair in front of his father's desk. A desk that had seemed to grow smaller over the years as Roderick grew into a man. When he was a boy, it had seemed so significant, taking up half the room. And now, it was just another desk. Just another few slabs of wood nailed together as it pretended to have powers it honestly didn't possess.

"What do you wish to talk to me about?" he asked his father, ignoring the desk as he looked up at the man standing near the drink cart in the corner.

"A stagecoach is arriving in town in the morning, and there is someone on it we must pick up."

"Who is it?"

His father said nothing as he moved over to the desk and sat down, setting his glass of iced tea on top after taking a rather large sip.

"Your new bride."

It was as though his father's words had punched him in the chest. Roderick sat forward, unable to catch a breath. "I beg your pardon."

"A young woman by the name of Lily Prescott is arriving tomorrow afternoon, and she is to be your new wife."

Roderick closed his eyes, shaking his head for a moment. "I'm sorry, but how do you know this woman?"

"I don't. I sent for her, and she is coming. I've been told she is a lovely woman."

"Ah, huh? And . . . I'm sorry, but I'm still failing to understand what is going on."

"When Emily Sanderson broke off your courtship, it was not just a blow to your heart. We have a reputation to uphold, even in Butte. You know of my dealings in the city, don't pretend that you don't. When word spreads of Emily's decision through all our friends, acquaintances, and business associates . . . well, I don't think I should have to explain to you the ramifications of it."

"And exactly what are the ramifications?"

"Weakness."

A bubble of anger simmered in Roderick's chest. He didn't understand why his love life—or lack thereof—was anyone's business but his own. And even if it was the business of his parents, it certainly wasn't the business of some acquaintance who lived dozens and dozens and dozens of miles away in another city.

"Now, you don't have to worry. I told Mr. Benson that our communication was strictly confidential. No one will know where she came from or how you two met. We could make up any story we want."

"Who is Mr. Benson?"

"He's the marriage broker."

"You sent for a mail-order bride?"

"Of course, I did. You know as well as I do that there aren't many eligible young women in Lone Hollow." His father leaned forward, resting his elbows on the desk. "She will stay in the guest house until we can plan a proper wedding, and then you two can stay there until I can have a house built somewhere on the property. I assume you wouldn't wish to keep the same plot of land Emily picked down by the lake. Perhaps we can let Miss Prescott choose."

"Or perhaps not." Roderick's brow furrowed, and he stood from the chair and paced the room. "I can't believe you think I would agree to this."

"Why wouldn't you?"

He stopped pacing and turned toward his father, resting his hands on his hips. "Are you insane?"

"And what is that supposed to mean? It would help if you had a bride and I sent for one. It's an easy fix."

"Oh, is that what it is? My heart is just an easy fix. I'm just supposed to fall at this woman's feet when she steps off the stagecoach tomorrow. Is that what is expected? It doesn't matter that I don't know what she looks like or the type of woman she is. It doesn't matter that she's a stranger to me. I'm just expected to love her instantly." He threw his hands up in the air and paced once more. "I'm sorry to disappoint you, Father, but none of that will be happening."

"I know what this may feel like, and it may feel like I'm asking the impossible—"

"You are. You are asking the impossible."

"No, I'm not. These types of arrangements have been going on for decades. Since the dawn of time, parents have married their children for the sake of the family's name."

"So, who is this woman, then? A Duchess or Countess of London who will make all your business problems go away? Or perhaps you've talked a princess into spending her life in Lone Hollow, a small town in the middle of nowhere, Montana." With the last of his words, his voice boomed once more, and he growled as he finished his sentence.

"I'm not sure of her background, but we will find out after she arrives, and we speak with her."

"I can't believe you are serious about this. You can't possibly think that I will just marry a stranger."

"Why not? If she is a lovely girl, then where lies the problem?"

Roderick stopped pacing and faced his father once more. He blinked at the man, wondering if his father had a stroke or whatever else could cause someone to lose their mind.

"I can't even believe you don't see the problem with this. Do you . . . are you siding with Emily? Do you agree with her reasons? Is that why you're doing this? Afraid that the only way a woman would marry your son now that he's got a horrible scar on his face is because she's forced to?"

"No. That's not why I sent for the girl."

"Then why did you send for her?"

"I told you why. Emily ending your courtship makes the

family's reputation look bad. It makes you look weak and unde-sirable."

"Perhaps I am. If you haven't noticed, I get stared at now whenever I go into town. I can't imagine what people are saying as I walk past them, whether to themselves or others. Look at the freak. What happened to him? Surely, they pray they never have to go through what I've been through. Surely, they thank God for the blessing that they don't look like me."

"You don't know what you're talking about. It's hardly noticeable."

"Oh, Father, you shouldn't tell lies. They are unbecoming."

As he turned to walk out of the office, his father jumped to his feet. "Don't you dare turn your back on me!" His voice boomed through the room, echoing off the walls and the windows.

Roderick stopped and faced his father once more. Before he could say anything, the door opened, and his mother strode in.

"What on earth is going on between you two? I could hear you down the hallway."

"Did you know about Father's master plan?" Roderick asked her.

"What plan?" She glanced between the two men as she folded her arms across her chest. Her brow furrowed.

"The plan to send for a mail-order bride."

Her mouth gaped open, and she moved toward her husband with her arm outstretched. She pointed her finger at his chest. "What on earth are you thinking?"

"I'm thinking about the boy's reputation now that Emily has broken things off with him. Do you have any idea what our friends and my business acquaintances are going to think when that girl gets married and our son is still a single man?"

"What do you mean when she gets married?" Roderick asked.

"I mean nothing by it other than that she is now an eligible young lady who will probably have a string of men to choose from."

"Whereas I have no one." Roderick rolled his eyes. "Just say what you mean, Father. It would do us all a lot better if you did."

"So, you thought a mail-order bride would be the answer?" His mother asked his father. "And you didn't think to tell me?"

"What is there to tell. She arrives tomorrow afternoon. Be ready to come into town to pick her up." Roderick's father strode out of the room with the last of his words, slamming the door behind him.

His mother inhaled a deep breath, letting it out slowly. "I will talk to him."

"I don't want to marry this girl, Mother."

"I know you don't, son. And you don't have to. I'll send her back to wherever she came from myself if I have to." She followed her husband, leaving Roderick alone in the office.

He felt like he was a little boy all over again, and his parents were deciding when and where he went to school. Was he not a grown man? Could he not make his own choices?

Well, I don't care what they think, he thought to himself. *I'm not marrying this young woman, no matter what she looks like or how lovely the letter says she is.*

THREE

LILY

*L*ily stepped off the stagecoach, and as the driver released her hand, she lifted it to her face to shield her eyes from the sun.

Lone Hollow.

She'd finally made it to the tiny town that had been on her mind for more years than she cared to admit. It was her father's town. Or at least, his last known area of residence. Whether he still lived here, she didn't know. A small part of her hoped he did, and yet there was also a part of her that feared the notion, too. How anyone could want something and not want something all at the same time, she didn't know. But that was where she was.

She wanted to find him.

And she didn't want to find him all at the same time.

"Here are your bags, Miss." The driver set her luggage at her feet.

"Thank you. Oh," she said, stopping him as he moved around her. "I'm sorry, but do you have the time?"

"No apologies needed, Miss. It's about an hour before noon."

"An hour before? But we were supposed to arrive at noon."

"Yes, Miss. We are early."

Early.

Figures.

Her stomach twisted, and it felt like butterflies were fluttering all around her insides. She didn't want to sit around the hotel for an hour waiting. Her nerves wouldn't allow it. She needed a distraction. At least for a little while.

"Excuse me, but do you know where I might find a cup of tea?"

The driver pointed off into the distance. "There's a café just down the street and around the corner. Not sure they serve tea, but you can get a good cup of coffee."

Coffee. Tea. What did it matter? It wasn't the drink she needed. It was the adventure of getting it she needed. Something to occupy her mind, and if it wasted a little time, that was a bonus.

"Thank you."

She scooped up her bags and headed down to the café.

Although a small town—or at least from what she could tell of it—the streets were busy with people. Some walking, some riding horses, and some driving wagons. They all seemed to zig and zag in different directions. A few of the men tipped their hats at her as she passed, while the women smiled and nodded. Most just ignored her completely, as their attention was far too focused on the children with them. Some older, some younger, and at least one of them were a newborn—or close to it— wrapped in a blanket and carried in his or her mother's arms.

Lily didn't want to think about how any of the men she'd passed could have been her father, and although she tried not to, there was a couple who caused her to pause a little and stare as though she was trying to see herself in their features.

Just stop, she thought to herself. *You can't think of that. Not right now.*

She grabbed the doorknob of the café, turning it before

opening the door and stepping inside, shaking her thoughts from her head.

"Top of the mornin' to yeh, Miss," a man greeted her. His Irish accent purred through his words.

"Good morning."

"What can I get yeh this mornin'?"

"Just a cup of coffee."

"Cream and sugar?"

"Yes, please."

"All right. Take a seat wherever yeh like. I'll bring it right over."

"Thank you."

She chose a seat in the corner near the window, hoping the view would ease the anxiousness she felt through her chest. She knew why she had to agree to this marriage, but the reasons did little to comfort the overwhelming notion she wasn't ready for any of it. She didn't know what exactly she'd done, agreeing to this, and she hated that it had been forced upon her.

"Here yeh go," the owner of the café set a cup in front of her along with another cup with cream and a tin full of sugar. "Care for anything else?"

"No. This is fine. Thank you."

As he strode away, she tucked her luggage near her feet under the table and rested her hands on her lap as she stared at the cup. Steam rose from the hot black liquid inside, and the aroma had a bitterness she could almost taste. After pouring in some cream and adding a few spoonfuls of sugar, she stirred it into a pale brown color and glanced out the window as she took a few sips. The warmth of the coffee ran down her throat and settled into her stomach.

"Did you hear about the Townsends and the Sandersons?" a man sitting at another table said. The other man in his company shook his head and shoveled a huge scoop of eggs into his mouth. He chewed a few bites, then swallowed and reached for his glass of water, sucking down a few gulps before responding.

Lily's ears perked up, too, hearing the name Townsend, and she fought against the instinct of glancing over at the men. Instead, she kept her eyes trained on the window.

"Nah, I didn't. What happened?"

"Apparently, Mr. Townsend and Mr. Sanderson had quite the falling out in his office the other day. The men could hear the shouting even down at the mill."

"What were they shouting about?"

"About the courtship of Mr. Sanderson's daughter with Mr. Townsend's son. I guess she ended it."

"Don't suppose I blame her."

Lily's brow furrowed at the man's words. Why wouldn't he blame her? Was there something about the young man that was bad? And bad enough for a woman to call off a courtship? Mr. Benson and Miss Whittaker had talked only about how lovely the young Mr. Townsend was. Had they been misinformed?

"I mean, any woman would have after what happened."

Lily shifted her head closer to the two men talking but kept her gaze on the table. What had happened? What were they talking about? The sudden realization she'd perhaps walked into a messy situation she might not be able to handle hit her like a mule kick to the chest. Her heart thumped, and her breath quickened.

"Mr. Townsend was quite angry over the whole thing. He thinks the young Mr. Townsend will have a reputation now."

"A reputation for what?" the other man asked.

"I don't know. Something about their business acquaintances in Butte. Who knows with those society men? They place far too much importance on clout."

Both men laughed, and the first one shook his head. "You can say that again. This is Lone Hollow. We don't care about none of that stuff."

The walls of the café closed in on Lily, and her breath quickened even more. What kind of a reputation did the young Mr. Townsend have? Was he an evil man? Did he harm this girl they spoke of?

So many questions ran through Lily's mind, and unfortunately, none of them would be answered. Not unless she asked the two men, and she certainly would not do that. Surely there had to be another way for her to stay at the orphanage. Perhaps she could apply for a job there. Become a headmistress herself. Or a maid. Or a cook. There had to be something for her to do. Anything. Anything except staying in this town and becoming the wife of a man who had done something to a girl that would give him a reputation.

She couldn't be here any longer. She needed to leave. And not just leave the café, she needed to leave Lone Hollow. This was a mistake. It was all a mistake, and if she just hurried, perhaps she could catch the stagecoach before it left. She didn't know what would happen when she arrived back at the orphanage, but it was a risk she was willing to take.

She shoved the chair away from the table and stood, and after grabbing her luggage, she made her way up to the counter, where the owner stood behind a large cash register reading a newspaper.

"What do I owe you?" she asked.

The man flipped the paper down and blinked. "Are . . . are you sure you're finished?"

The bell above the door chimed, but she ignored it along with the gentle breeze that blew in from the outside, moving her long blonde curls and the skirt of her dress. "Yes, I'm sure. How much is the bill?"

"Well, it's ten cents, Miss."

A nervous flutter washed through her whole body, and she opened her handbag, fumbling inside for change to pay for the coffee. Her hands slipped on the leather, and the handbag tumbled to the ground, spilling the contents on the floor. She bent down to gather her things, and as she reached for an old locket that her mother had given her, another hand grasped it and scooped it up.

"What are you—" She glanced up, meeting a pair of chocolate eyes set in an oval, handsome face, "doing," she finished.

The young man smiled and handed her the locket. "I just thought I would help. I'm not trying to steal it."

"My apologies. I didn't mean to sound as though I thought you were."

"No apologies are needed. Let me help you." He bent down again, grabbing the last few coins that had fallen out and scattered on the floor. He handed everything to her, and as he shifted his weight and turned his head, sunlight glinted across his face, exposing a scar that ran from his hairline down to his chin. It gave him a rugged look and almost made him more attractive than he would have been without it.

She took her belongings and smiled. "Thank you."

After putting everything back into her bag, she handed the café owner a dime and collected her luggage. The young man tipped his hat, and she gave him a nod, glancing at him one last time as she left the café, letting the door close behind her. For a moment, she almost forgot why she'd left the café so quickly.

To leave, she remembered, and she dashed off toward the hotel. With any luck, she could still catch the stagecoach.

RODERICK

*R*oderick didn't want to glance after the young woman, but as he caught her trotting past the window out of the corner of his eye, he couldn't help but turn to watch her. There was something different about her. Something he couldn't put his finger on. It was as though she looked at him instead of his scar—which wasn't something he'd seen in a while. The line down his face had become the first thing people stared at.

But her?

She looked into his eyes first, last, and her gaze hardly left him the whole time they were near.

"Good mornin', Mr. Townsend," Jeremiah said. "What can I get yeh this morning?"

"Huh? Oh. Nothing." He backed away from the counter, shaking his head. "I'm fine. I thought I needed coffee, but . . . actually, do you know who that young woman was?"

Jeremiah shook his head. "Can't say that I do, Mr. Townsend. She came in and ordered coffee. But I don't think she finished it before she paid and left." The Irishman nodded toward the table in the corner, where a cup still sat on top. Steam rose from the coffee still inside it.

"Well, thank you." Roderick tipped his hat. "I best be on my way."

By the time he'd made it back out to the street, the young woman had vanished, and as he made his way back to the hotel to meet his father, the once few questions he'd had about the stranger had doubled. Who was she? And why had she left in such a hurry? Questions he knew he would never get the answers to, but questions he asked himself just the same.

Although why he did, he didn't know. It was pointless. Pointless because not only did he not know who the girl was, but because he was headed to the hotel to meet the woman his father sent for. The mail-order bride he was supposed to marry and the mail-order bride he wanted nothing to do with.

Anger bubbled in his chest as the reminder of why he was in town flooded back into his mind. He scaled the stairs to the hotel, taking off his hat as he reached for the doorknob and opened the door. A slight growl vibrated through him.

"Son. Over here," his father called out. He spun to face the man, biting back a smart remark as his father stepped aside and revealed the young woman from the café standing in front of him.

"You." Roderick pointed at her.

"Hello," she said, extending her hand. "I'm Lily. Lily Prescott."

FOUR

LILY

*A*fter getting settled into the guest house at the Townsend estate, Lily sat on the edge of the bed, staring out the window. She'd been here once before. Not here as in this place, but here as in the feeling of being in an unknown place with no idea of what the future held.

She hated this feeling.

It lacked control and it lacked stability. It was as though she was spinning around and around, and she didn't have the power to stop herself. Her life had been one decision after another, but unfortunately, they were decisions she didn't make. Someone else always chose for her. Telling her what to do, where to go, and what would happen.

Yes, she hated this feeling more than anything else in her existence.

And being here was just another one of those choices made by someone else.

How could I have missed the stagecoach, she thought to herself. She'd left the café in Lone Hollow, believing that God would answer her prayers and the stagecoach would still be in front of the hotel.

It wasn't.

And she knew as she climbed the stairs that her fate was set. She'd become the wife of a young man who, as the strangers said and she overheard, had an unknown reputation.

A knock rapped on the door, and as she opened it, Roderick met her with a slight smile. Her heart thumped.

"How are the accommodations?" he asked.

"They are all right."

"Just all right?" He raised one eyebrow, and his tone had a hint of amusement.

Had she said something wrong? "The guest house is beautiful. Is that what you wanted to know?" she asked.

His smile vanished, and he ducked his chin. "No, I suppose 'it's all right' is fine. I've . . . I've come to invite you to dinner this evening with my parents and me. In the main house, of course."

"All right."

"Six o'clock."

She nodded. "I'll be there."

***

Lily didn't know what she dreaded more—being in Lone Hollow in the first place or having dinner with the Townsends. Although she supposed it would be a chance to get to know, her future husband and his family, a part of her wondered if she wanted to know them. She didn't want to think about how her gut was telling her they weren't what they made themselves out to be to Mr. Benson, nor what she would do when and if the truth came out.

Ignoring how her anxiousness crawled along her skin, she scaled the stairs and crossed the porch of the main house, entering the door and closing it behind her. It wasn't a tiny house by any means, but it wasn't overly large either. A nice size, the hardwood floors were stained a deep rich color—like that of the chocolate sweet Miss Whittaker would surprise the children at the orphanage with on Christmas morning, and they played off the white painted walls covered in different paintings of landscapes. Forests, ponds, even a meadow. She stared at them all as she passed, letting her thoughts drift off to the unknown places and how she would give anything to be in those paintings instead of in the house.

Footsteps thumped down the hallway, and she turned to see Roderick approaching her. He smiled. "Follow me."

She did as he asked and followed him down the hallway and into the dining room. The table had already been set, and as she entered the room, Mr. Townsend, Roderick's father, stood from his chair. The woman, whom she assumed was his mother, didn't.

"Ah. Miss Prescott. Welcome."

She smiled and nodded but said nothing.

"Have a seat," Mr. Townsend pointed toward a chair next to his son, and as they took their seats, he returned to his own. The three of them grabbed their napkins, and as they shook them open and laid them in their laps, Lily fetched hers, mimicking their movement. "I don't believe you've had the chance to meet my wife. This is Roderick's mother, Caroline."

"It's a pleasure to meet you," she said to the woman.

The woman nodded but made no effort to speak or smile at Lily.

"I trust that the guest house is to your liking?" Mr. Townsend asked her.

"Yes, it's . . . lovely." She tucked her arms into her lap, fighting to straighten her shoulders. An old habit of slouching had always been her nemesis and one Miss Whittaker fought daily.

"I hope you like the stew," Roderick said to her, pointing at a steaming pot in the middle of the table. He reached for it, offering for her to take the ladle and serve herself.

She did.

"It smells wonderful."

"I'm sure you must be famished after your travels."

"Yes, it was quite the long journey." She dug the ladle down into the thick broth, scooping out two servings and dumping them into her bowl.

When she was finished, Roderick served himself and passed the pot to his mother, who mirrored them and handed it to his father.

"So, where are you from?" Mr. Townsend asked.

"Butte."

"And do your parents still live there?" his mother asked.

A lump formed in Lily's throat, and although she tried to swallow it, it wouldn't budge. "No. My mother passed away when I was just a little girl, and I don't know where my father is."

Mrs. Townsend's eyes narrowed, and her brow furrowed. "So, where did you grow up? And with whom?"

"In the orphanage." Hesitation and confusion burned through Lily's mind as she answered Mrs. Townsend's question. Did they not know anything about her? Had Mr. Benson not sent them word about where he had acquired her?

Mrs. Townsend's mouth gaped open, and she glanced at her husband. "You not only sent for a mail-order bride for your son, but you didn't even have the sense to make sure she was a proper lady of society!" The more her words came out of her mouth, the higher her tone became, and by the time she finished, she was shouting at the top of her lungs.

Lily sucked in a deep breath, holding it until her body begged her to let it go. Her eyes widened, and her blood ran cold through her veins. She'd seen Miss Whittaker yell at a child once or twice, but never had she ever witnessed such a tone or volume on another person.

"Calm down, Caroline," Mr. Townsend.

"I will not calm down, Zachary. How could you do this?"

"Do what? She's a lovely girl." Mr. Townsend lifted his hand, motioning toward Lily. She closed her eyes for a moment, then fixed her gaze on the plate in front of her. She hated being talked about like she wasn't in the room, but she knew the feeling well after years in the orphanage. "She's pretty, and she seems to have decent manners. She speaks when spoken to and carries herself like any other lady I've known."

"That's not the point." Mrs. Townsend balled her hand into a fist and slammed it down on the table. The glasses of water sitting in front of all of them shook, and the water rippled. "She's an orphan. What are we going to tell our friends? They will want to know where she is from and who her parents are."

"Tell them whatever you want."

Lily sucked in a breath. She hadn't known her mother's death would have such an effect on her life. It wasn't that she chose it. She didn't choose for her mother to die, and her mother certainly didn't choose to die and leave her daughter on this earth alone.

"Mother, could we perhaps finish this discussion after eating?" Roderick glanced at his mother, then at Lily for a moment.

Lily's breath quickened.

"Who left you at the orphanage?" Mrs. Townsend asked.

Lily flinched. "My mother. Right before she died." She looked up, meeting the woman's hard stare. "It wasn't her choice to leave me there. She didn't want that for me."

"And your father? You said you don't know where he is. Why?"

"My mother never told me about him."

Mrs. Townsend rolled her eyes, exhaling a deep breath. "And what did your mother do for work?"

"She was a seamstress."

"A seamstress? Are you sure?"

"Yes. Why do you ask?"

"Well, child, it stands to reason that a woman who doesn't

know about their child's father isn't exactly . . . how should I put this? Usually, a woman, who doesn't know the man who fathered their child, has unquestionable morals."

"Are you saying she worked . . . she worked . . ." No matter how many times Lily tried to say the next word, she couldn't. So, she didn't. Instead, she straightened her shoulders and gave a hard stare in return. "My mother was a seamstress. I used to visit the dress shop where she worked," she said flatly.

"Mother, please. I must ask again that we discuss all of this after dinner."

Mrs. Townsend blinked at her son for a moment. "Are you saying you are all right with this?"

"All right with what?"

"You were more than disagreeable with this situation just yesterday and this morning. What happened?"

Roderick opened his mouth but then shut it and dropped his gaze for a moment. It was as though he was collecting himself before he said something he would later regret.

"Mother, I'm not saying I condone this. All I'm asking for is to discuss it after dinner." His voice lowered into a deepness by the end.

"Well, I don't want to wait until after dinner to discuss this." She turned to her husband. "Zachary, you have made nothing but a mess of this situation. You bring in a young girl who is not worthy of our son at all, and you think I should bite my tongue or that Roderick should accept it. I won't have it."

Lily ducked her chin even further into her chest. Her eyes were misted with tears, yet she fought them with every ounce of strength. She didn't want to allow this woman the satisfaction of knowing she'd made Lily cry. Nor did she need any more judgment. She didn't know if this woman would consider crying weak.

"I just don't know what I'm going to tell my friends." She threw her hands up in the air.

"Well, you better figure out something because she is staying, and the invitation I received this afternoon is why she is staying."

"What invitation?" Mrs. Townsend asked.

"It's an invitation to the engagement party for a Miss Emily Sanderson and a Mr. Stewart Dowery."

"Dowery? As in Matthew Dowery, the bank mogul?"

"Yes, that Mr. Dowery." Mr. Townsend rested his forearms on the table, exhaling a deep breath with his words.

"Emily is engaged?" Roderick gaped at his father, ignoring his mother's shock.

"Yes, son. She is."

"But . . . they just moved to Butte. She just ended our courtship a couple of months ago." His voice rose into a near shout, and Lily ducked her chin even more.

This had to be, without a doubt, the worst dinner party she'd ever been to. And it didn't even matter that this was also probably the first dinner party she'd ever been to. She felt like a nine-year-old all over again, sitting at a table where others talked about her life as though they were in control of her life.

"I understand your anger, son, but that doesn't change the fact that she's engaged, and we've been invited to the engagement party."

"But all of Butte society will be there. They will know what she did to our son."

"Not unless he comes with another woman on his arm."

Lily felt three pairs of eyes suddenly upon her. She didn't look up; however, she just stared at her dinner, which had stopped steaming a while ago. Now she would also have to endure a cold supper, too.

"Her background doesn't matter. Dress her in a nice dress, and she will look lovely on our son's arm. No one will know her. You can make up any story you like and perhaps even make her a more suitable sounding match than Emily Sanderson would have been for this family. I don't care what that story is, I will leave it up to you, but the fact remains that she stays, and the marriage between Roderick and this woman will happen." Mr. Townsend threw his napkin onto his bowl and shoved his chair away from the table. A slight growl left his lips as he stormed out of the dining room, leaving the three of them in his wake. Roderick sat for a moment with a far-off look to his eyes as though lost in thought, and while he didn't move for a bit, he soon threw his napkin down and left the room in the same manner.

Lily's heart thumped. Left alone with the woman who seemed to hate her the most, she didn't know what to do or say, and she prayed with every ounce of her that Mrs. Townsend would leave without another word.

Fortunately, her prayers were answered, and the woman only glared at her for a moment, narrowing her eyes before she, too, set her napkin on her bowl and left.

Finally, alone in the room, Lily took a breath, grabbed several rolls from the plate in the middle of the table, and darted for the front door and the safety of the guest house. Tears streamed down her cheeks.

This was nothing more than the biggest mistake anyone had made for her in her whole life. This was even worse than her mother leaving her at the orphanage.

FIVE

LILY

*S*till reeling from the dinner disaster the night before, Lily headed down to the barn. She couldn't spend another minute pacing through the guest house while the conversation last night replayed in her mind, and although she wasn't sure if she was allowed in the barn, she didn't care. She needed space. She needed air.

She needed a distraction.

The early morning sunlight filtered through the windows around the horse stalls, and as she walked down the breezeway, a few of the four-legged animals came to the stall doors to greet her. Two were brown, one was black, and another was a yellow-ish-brown with a black mane and tail, and that one nickered to her as it stopped at the stall door. She made her way over to the horse, touching the side of its face, and as it lowered its head, she ran her fingers over its ears, through the hair laying on its forehead and down the face.

"Do you know anything about horses?" a voice asked.

She sucked in a breath and spun to face Mrs. Townsend approaching from the barn's entrance.

She shook her head. "I'm afraid I don't."

"That's all right. I don't expect you would, growing up in a home for unwanted children."

"I wasn't unwanted. My mother died."

"I suppose you have a point." Mrs. Townsend folded her arms across her chest. "You should learn about them. If you are going to stay here, that is." The woman moved toward Lily, motioning toward the horse she was petting. "That one belongs to Mr. Townsend, along with that one over there." She gestured toward one Lily hadn't seen yet and who now looked out of its stall, blinking at the visitors.

"That one," Mrs. Townsend pointed to the black one, "she is mine, and those two are Roderick's."

"You have a lot of horses," Lily said, continuing to pet the one in front of her.

"Roderick and Zachary have a lot of horses. I have one, and that is enough."

"You sound like you don't like them."

"I don't mind them. But I don't see the need for them."

"Not even to pull the wagons?"

Mrs. Townsend shrugged. "I suppose they have some purpose." She paused, glancing over her shoulder as she clicked her tongue. "Do you wish to ride one?"

Lily sucked in a breath, nearly choking as her spit hit the back of her throat. "Me? Ride one? No. I don't wish . . ."

"Oh, it's easy. Besides, you're going to have to learn. It might as well be now. You are here. I am here. I can help you."

Hesitation purred through Lily's chest. With all the things this woman had said about her not even a day ago, why did she wish to help her now? It made little sense.

"Oh, no. You don't have to . . . we can . . . I can learn later. I'm sure you must have lots of stuff to do. You don't need to waste any time on me."

"It's not wasting time if it's for my son's future wife." Mrs. Townsend cocked one eyebrow, and her lips twitched into a scowl after she said the word wife. Her expression twisted in Lily's gut, and Lily knew she needed to get out of the situation.

"I think there is plenty of time for me to learn. Really. You do not need to bother yourself with it today." Lily backed away with her hands up, but Mrs. Townsend moved toward her, stopping her.

"Don't think you are getting away that easy. You are doing this today." The woman waved her hand, and, ignoring Lily's retreat, she made her way across the barn, fetching some rope that she tied around a horse's neck before walking it out into the breezeway of the barn.

A lump formed in Lily's throat. She gulped at it the whole time she watched Mrs. Townsend brush the horse, then place a blanket, saddle, and stuck a piece of steel or iron in its mouth.

"It's called a bit and bridle," Mrs. Townsend said, hooking the straps of leather over the horse's ears.

"I don't know if I even remember that." A whispered giggle left Lily's lips.

Mrs. Townsend finished buckling the bridle and handed her the reins. "Don't worry. You'll get the hang of it."

"What do I do now?" Lily asked.

"Lead the horse out of the barn, of course."

Lily inhaled a deep breath and started walking toward the barn doors. The horse followed her, and although she wanted to stop every few steps to try to calm her heartbeat, thumping hard in her chest or slow her breathing, she didn't. She actually didn't stop until she reached outside.

Mrs. Townsend checked the strap around the belly then stepped back. "Well, you're all set."

"Thank you." Lily approached the horse's side. "This saddle isn't like any I've seen before."

"No, I wouldn't imagine you have. This is a lady's saddle. You're meant to ride sidesaddle as all proper ladies should ride. Not like a man with one leg on each side." Mrs. Townsend moved toward the saddle, pointing to different parts. "This is the leaping head and the fixed head, and they will keep you secure in the saddle." She turned and pointed over toward a large tree stump. "I always use that to get on. Just stick your foot in the stirrup and hoist yourself up. Your right leg goes here, and your left leg goes here."

Lily gulped again and led the horse over to the stump, climbing on how Mrs. Townsend instructed her. Out of balance, she teetered on the back of the horse and a tensed fear washed through her body. She walked the horse around in a few circles and stopped, inhaling a deep breath to help calm herself.

It only worked a little.

"You are doing simply fine. I think it's time to see what you can do,"

"What? Wait. No." Lily turned slightly to the side as Mrs. Townsend picked up a nearby stick and smacked the horse on the rump.

The horse bolted, and the reins flew out of Lily's hands as she reached forward and grabbed the mane with one hand and the saddle with the other. She leaned forward and down on the horse's neck, trying to find her balance as the horse took off across the pasture and into the trees around the house.

Lily screamed, and the horse seemed to go even faster. It galloped down a path through the trees, weaving left, then right as it ran. Lily clung to the saddle and the mane, and each time she tried to reach for the reins, her balance would slip, and she abandoned her quest to reach for the strips of leather just to stay on.

The horse sped faster and faster through the trees. Its lungs heaved, and its breathing sounded like a freight train.

"Stop! Please, stop! Horse," she said to it.

It didn't listen.

"Please. Just stop. Why won't you stop?"

A log lay in the middle of the trail up ahead, and Lily closed her eyes for a moment, not wanting to think about how the horse would either veer around it or, worse, jump right over it. She leaned forward, trying to hide her face in the mane that was whipping in the air from the movement.

"Please, don't." She closed her eyes again. Stride after stride, she could feel the speed building, and as she opened her eyes, the horse's front legs left the ground, and it sailed over the log. As the front legs landed and the back legs were still in the air, the force pitched her out of the saddle, and she flew, landing on the ground with a thud. Her body rolled several times, then stopped, and she landed flat on her back. Pain shot through her whole body, and dirt-caked her face. She coughed and sputtered as she struggled to breathe.

The horse galloped off, and the thundering hoofprints soon faded. Lily laid still on the ground, looking up at the trees and the view of the sky flecking through the branches. She knew she needed to get up, but it was the last thing she wanted to do. Instead, she wanted to lie there forever. Or at least until she died. Then her bones could lay there forever.

Tears misted her eyes. She didn't want to think that Mrs. Townsend had done this on purpose, but her gut feeling was that the woman had. And now it wasn't just a verbal attack she'd had to endure from Roderick's mother, but now a physical one, too.

Hooves pounded the ground in the distance. They sounded as though a horse was just walking, however, and Lily hesitated on looking up to see who was coming. She didn't want to see Mrs. Townsend's face.

"Miss Prescott?" Roderick's voice asked.

Lily closed her eyes. While she hadn't wanted to see Mrs. Townsend, she also hadn't wanted to see Roderick either. Her hope that it would have been a stranger dashed.

"Miss Prescott, are you all right?"

She heard the squeaking sounds of leather as though he was

dismounting his horse, and before she could react, he appeared in her vision, standing over her as he looked down upon her. "Miss Prescott?"

"I'm all right."

"Well, at least you have that going for you. May I ask you what you are doing out here?"

Heat flushed through her cheeks, and she blinked as she trained her gaze on the trees above her instead of on him.

"Oh, you know, just pondering life, I suppose." It was the only thing she could think to say without casting ill will toward the man's mother.

"So, you went for a walk and just lay in the middle of the trail?"

Before she could answer, she heard another horse galloping toward them and past them, and she caught the sight of the horse she'd been riding run past, headed back to the Townsend property and back to the barn. They both watched the horse until it vanished.

"Not exactly," she said to him.

SIX

RODERICK

*R*oderick held out his hand for Lily to take, and he helped her to her feet, stepping away from her a little as she brushed the dirt and twigs from the skirt of her dress.

"Are you sure you aren't hurt?" he asked.

She shook her head. "I'm all right."

"What were you doing riding my mother's horse?"

Lily bit her lip and ducked her chin. He got the distinct impression it was a question she didn't want to answer.

"Did my mother put you up to it?"

She nodded, keeping her gaze focused on the ground. It had been the answer that, while he knew was coming, he'd hoped it wasn't true. He knew the mare his mother had picked, and he was almost shocked Lily had stayed on for as long as she did.

"They trained the mare to run. She runs from the barn, down the trail, around the meadow, then back to the barn. That's all the riding my mother does, so that's all the mare knows."

"So, your mother knew this would happen."

He inhaled a deep breath. "Yes, I'm afraid she did."

Lily's shoulders hunched slightly for a moment; then, she straightened them. "Well, I suppose I should get back to the guest house and wash up. I wouldn't want to be further accused of being *improper or unworthy of you.*" A hint of annoyance bubbled in her tone, and she rolled her eyes as she finished her sentence.

"May I walk with you?" he asked.

She stared at him for a moment, then shrugged. "If that is your wish."

He followed her for a little while before settling into a pace next to her. Although he glanced at her a few times, she never looked at him. Instead, she kept her attention on either the trail in front of them or the trees off in the distance. He didn't want to believe that she was ignoring him on purpose, but the farther they walked without saying a word, the more he did.

He cleared his throat. "I'm sorry for last night.'

"What about it?"

"For what they said."

"Why are you sorry? You said nothing."

"I know. But what my mother did say . . . it was uncalled for."

Lily glanced away from him and stared off in the other direction for a long time. He waited for her to say something—anything—but after several minutes of her silence, he continued.

"I want you to know her anger . . . it wasn't about you. It was about Emily Sanderson and me." He paused again, waiting for her to ask about Emily. She didn't. "Emily and I were courting, and I would have proposed. She broke it off, though." Again, he paused. Lily still stared at the trees as she folded her arms across her chest. "Do you not have any questions?" he asked.

She finally glanced at him. "Honestly, I don't care to know anything about your family. Your father has shown me kindness—"

"I have too."

She opened her mouth but shut it for a moment before she spoke. "I suppose you have. However, I heard about you from the men in the café. How you caused that woman to break it off with you."

"You heard what?" His head whipped toward her, and he blinked.

"I don't remember what they said, but they made it sound as though it was your fault."

"My fault? She ended it because she didn't want a husband with this." He stopped walking and pointed toward the scar on his face. "She ended it because she couldn't handle looking at me. She broke it off because she couldn't love me enough to see past my accident and the scar it left behind."

Lily stopped walking and turned to face him. Her shoulders seemed to soften, and she glanced down at the ground for a moment before meeting his gaze.

"My apologies for my mistake."

"It's all right. I can see how overhearing something about someone you don't know can give you a jaded perspective of them."

She nodded, ducking her chin once more, and they both continued walking down the trail. His horse followed close behind, lowering its head with the slow pace of the humans on foot.

"Do you mind if I ask what happened?" she asked him.

"A blade came loose, sliced into my face. The doctors stitched it as best they could, but they couldn't keep it from leaving the scar."

"I'm sorry you had to go through that."

"And I'm sorry you had to go through the pain of your mother dying and leaving you in an orphanage."

They both looked at each other, holding each other's gazes for a moment. He smiled, and she smiled in return before she refocused on the trail ahead of them. A calmness seemed to wash through the both of them as though the tension had eased after they had finally spoken words they needed to, to one another. While he didn't know if such was a truth for her, he knew it was a truth for him.

Well, almost.

"I will speak to my mother about her behavior and treatment of you," he said. "I don't know why she believes she can behave in such a manner. But I will tell her to stop."

"Thank you."

They continued in silence. A few questions plagued his mind, and although he wanted to ask them, he didn't know if he should. Or perhaps it was he didn't know if he wanted to know her thoughts.

"May I ask something?"

"No one is stopping you."

He smiled. "I have to say I do enjoy the little fire you sometimes have. But I've also noticed that there are other times when I expect you to speak up for yourself, and yet you don't."

"As in?"

"Last night. You sat at the table and said not a single word. And yet, now, you have no problem showing me there is a hint of boldness to you."

"Perhaps it was knocked into me when I hit the ground after falling off the horse."

He snorted at her tone. It was annoyed with a hint of anger and playfulness. As though she wanted to joke but held so much truth to her words, they were no joke at all.

"So, what is it you wanted to ask me?" She glanced at him.

A rock hit the pit of his stomach and rolled around for a moment as he inhaled and exhaled a deep breath. "Are you . . . did you want to come to Lone Hollow?"

Lily hesitated for a moment, and the rock in his stomach pitched and rolled even more. He didn't exactly know what he wanted her answer to be, and the thought of either yes or no . . . he didn't know how to respond. If she said yes, did that mean she wanted to marry a stranger? And if she did, were her feelings still the same after what his mother had done and after she saw him —the real him, scar and all. On the other side of that, should she say no, did that mean she was forced? And if so, how did she feel now? Did she feel the same way now and not wish to marry him?

The sheer number of questions that crept into his mind was maddening, and he fought the anxious itch by pressing his fingers into the back of his neck while he waited for her answer. His fingers strained from the pressure and hurt.

"To be honest," she said, giving him a sideways glance. "I had to come. The Headmistresses at the orphanage . . . they wanted me to leave since I was no longer a child. Miss Whittaker knew I had no place to go, so when Mr. Benson, the marriage broker, wrote to her, she wrote him back about me."

"So, it wasn't your choice?"

"No, it wasn't."

Guilt simmered in his chest. He had only thought of how his father's intentions had affected him. He hadn't thought of how they had affected her. He didn't want to imagine what the last few days had been like for her. Plucked out of the only home she'd ever known, after losing her mother at such a young age, and sent away to live with strangers until she was forced to marry one of them. And he didn't want to analyze how she must have felt, knowing all of this, to have her worth be questioned in the way his mother had done last night. And to then be forced upon the back of a horse, which she didn't know, and sent galloping down the trail . . .

"And now? Is it your choice to stay?"

"I don't feel it is. I feel like it's your mother's."

"But if it wasn't up to her, and it was up to you, would you stay?"

"I don't know." She looked up at him. Her eyes were piercing into his. "But if I didn't, it wouldn't be because of your scar."

He opened his mouth but shut it as they emerged from the trees, and the house and barn came into their view. He could see his mother standing at the fence, and as he glanced at Lily, she ducked her chin and pressed her lips together.

Anger bubbled in his chest. He rarely opposed his mother, but this . . . Lily . . . she was something different. Whether or not she stayed and whether or not he even wanted her to stay, none of that mattered. He needed to speak to his mother. Now.

"I would see you back to the guest house, but I need to speak with my mother," he said to Lily.

She nodded but only moved her chin toward him, not looking at him at all. "Have a pleasant afternoon," she whispered before striding off for the safety of the guest house.

He watched her for a moment, then exhaled a deep breath as he made his way over to the barn.

"I don't know what happened," his mother said as he approached. "She told me she could handle a horse, so I thought nothing of putting her on Princess, thinking she could breeze down the trail, through the meadow, and back to the barn."

"Is that so?"

Her face twisted with a scowl. "Do you doubt me?"

"I don't know what to believe or doubt with you anymore, Mother. But I do know this . . . whatever it is you are trying to do to that poor girl will stop."

"I don't know what you're talking—"

"She's a human being, Mother. She's not a toy or anything you can play with and discard when you don't want anymore. Now, you have made your opinions perfectly clear. However, they are your opinions. They aren't mine."

"Are you saying you wish to marry the girl?"

"No. I'm not saying that. I don't know if I want to. But whether or not I do, it's my choice. And if I decide I do, you need to respect that choice. And it would help if you respected her. She is the most innocent out of this whole mess."

"Innocent? I don't understand."

"She didn't want to come to Lone Hollow. She was forced to."

"Well, then she shouldn't mind it if we send her back to Butte."

"She can't go back. She has nowhere to go."

His mother rolled her eyes. "Of course. It sounds just like your father to not think his plans through or to do a poor job of it."

"I don't know if I would say that."

"Well, I would." Mother folded her arms across her chest as she glanced toward the guest house. She cocked one of her legs out and tapped her foot on the ground. "I wonder if I gave her money . . ."

"After what you did today with the horse, I don't want you going near her again. At least not until I figure things out."

She gaped at him. "I didn't do anything—"

"Don't lie. You've never been good at it. Just leave Miss Prescott alone." He turned to leave, and his mother reached out, grabbing the sleeve of his jacket. "Where are you going?"

"I'm going to fix the mess you created today. I only hope it's enough to make the poor girl feel comfortable here."

"So, you want to marry her?"

"I never said that. But marriage or not, I at least want her mind at ease while she's here." Before his mother could say another word, he strode off, a slight growl on his lips. He didn't know how he felt about the young lady. Could he see himself with her for the rest of his life? Perhaps. But he had seen the same in Emily, and he knew how that had turned out. He didn't want to go through another breakup.

Ever again.

SEVEN

RODERICK

*R*oderick hadn't known how to make up for what his mother had done. But he figured getting Lily out of the guest house for an afternoon and taking her on a tour of the sawmill might be a pleasant change for her. At least for a day, and at least he hoped.

What he hadn't counted on, however, was for how loud the sawmill would be to her or how scared she would be of it.

Well, interested, but still scared.

"I'm sorry if this doesn't interest you," he said, his voice at a near shout over the engine.

Lily held her hands over her ears as she stood next to him. Her eyes were wide as the logs ran through the blade, and she flinched at the noises. "What?" she asked.

"I said, I'm sorry if this doesn't interest you."

She removed one hand from her ear, pointing to it. "I can't hear you."

He motioned for her to move away from the mill by placing his hand on the small of her back. Her body moved with his touch, and as they settled into a less noisy area, they stopped.

"Is that better?" he asked.

"Yes. Much."

"I said I'm sorry if this doesn't interest you." He shoved his hands in his pockets and pointed his chin toward the mill.

"Honestly, it is interesting. I never knew how logs were cut, and I would love to keep watching. It's just . . . It's just . . . loud." She brushed her fingertips across her forehead. "I'm surprised the men don't get headaches."

"Oh, they do. I guess you just learn to live with them." He withdrew his pocket watch from his jacket pocket, checking the time. "They should shut down here in a few minutes. It's lunchtime, and the children and wives will arrive soon."

"For what?"

"For lunch. Most of the men have families who bring their lunch to them every day. Then they eat together."

"Well, that's nice."

"Yeah. I brought ours too. That's what was in the basket. Are you hungry?"

"I could eat."

She nodded and smiled, and he noticed how his heart thumped at the way her face lit up a little with her smile. He still was unsure if he wanted her to stay or if he wanted to marry her; however, he also didn't want her feeling uncomfortable. He knew how that felt, and he didn't wish that upon anyone. Even a total stranger who had been brought here to ward off a poor reputation for him. He didn't want to think of that, though.

"Great. I know of the perfect picnic spot."

LILY

*B*y the time they had made it down near the pond, the man had shut down the mill. While he set out the blanket and the food, Lily watched the women and children arrive. A sense of family and happiness warmed through them as they all embraced. It was as though the men had been waiting for this time of day ever since they arrived at work this morning.

Perhaps they had.

It was one of the few times she'd witnessed such closeness like that. Or at least since her mother died. In the years she lived with her mother, she'd known more love than she could carry in her mind. However, after her mother died, she would only ever see loving hugs when children were adopted, and the family came to pick them up. She'd watch with the other children at the top of the stairs. Their faces all peered through the rails of the railing as they peered down on the husband and wife, hugging their new child and telling them how they were going to love them forever and how they were going to do everything to make the child feel at home.

It was always a bittersweet moment for her, as she always wanted the other children to find homes, and she wanted it for herself, too. At times it had been hard to see, and yet, even in those times, she always tried to remain hopeful. At least until now.

"It's ready," Roderick said behind her, and she turned to see a lovely picnic spread.

"It looks delicious."

She sat on the ground, tucking her legs up as she smoothed out the skirt of her dress. "I used to love picnics as a child. It's been a while since I've had one."

"Really?"

"Miss Whittaker always tried to plan fun outings for the children. But as I grew older . . . it was more for the little ones."

"My grandfather always said fresh air does good for the body." Roderick sat on the ground across from her and propped an elbow on his knee. "Because of this, I think the man ate more meals outside than he did inside."

"I suppose I would believe that. I've always felt better after being outside. Perhaps it has something to do with the sun too."

"Yeah, I think that adds to it."

"So, how long has the sawmill been in your family?"

"For five generations. My father hopes that it remains for several more." A slight groan vibrated through his chest.

"You don't sound as though you hold the same thoughts as your father."

"Is it that obvious?"

She chuckled, and he couldn't help but notice the tension in her shoulders eased. "Only a little," she said. "Why don't you?"

"I wanted to go to university after my schooling, not work the sawmill."

"And what did you want to study?"

"To be a lawyer."

Lily didn't know why, but she couldn't help but picture him dressed in a smart suit and standing in some courthouse in some city, pacing as he defended his client. Although she didn't know what a courtroom looked like, she'd heard stories from other children who did.

She opened her mouth to say as much but thought better of it and silenced herself before she said a word. Why encourage him in such a manner when it obviously would never happen?

"It is a fine job," he continued, fetching a plate for her, filling it with some assorted crackers, cheese, and fruit. "An important job. Being a lawyer."

"Yes, I know it is."

"But so is the sawmill. People need lumber to build homes for their families. I suppose, in a way, I still help and contribute to society. That's all I've ever wanted to do."

"Well, for what it's worth, I don't think you should downplay the sawmill. Homes are important to people. Perhaps one of the most important things. Take your men, for example." She pointed toward the lot of them all sitting around with their wives and children, stuffing their faces with sandwiches. "They seem to love their families. Surely, they wouldn't want them to be homeless."

"I see your point." He chuckled and ducked his chin. "I still would have liked to have studied law."

"I understand. I wish I could have studied medicine."

He blinked, and his mouth gaped. "Medicine?"

"Yes. I've always found it fascinating, and to heal someone . . . I would think there be no greater thrill." Her smile faded. "But there is no place for a woman in medicine."

"There are a few women doctors, aren't there?"

"I've read about a couple. But they are also not orphans. They grew up with money and opportunities. Don't get me wrong, I commend them, and I hope they do extraordinarily well. I just wish I could join them."

He nodded, and although he said nothing, she could tell he understood how she felt. Both of them were tied to futures they didn't pick for themselves, and while it was sad, they still knew they had a role in their lives.

Or at least that is what she thought. She wasn't entirely sure about him.

"Excuse me, Mr. Townsend?" a voice asked.

Both Lily and Roderick glanced up at one wife standing over their blanket and them.

"Sorry to interrupt, Mr. Townsend," the woman said.

"You aren't."

"It's just the kids and me, and well, we brought Luke way too much to eat today. He left for work this morning so early, and I had yet to make him a proper breakfast. I thought for sure he'd be starving, so I made him extra for lunch. Well, I went and made him too much, and . . . well, I noticed you have a mighty fine spread here, but I just thought I'd offer y'all some home-made potato salad. I have some beans too. If y'all are interested."

Lily glanced between the woman and Roderick. He said

nothing but shrugged at her as if to tell her it was her choice. Not wishing to be rude to the woman and itching for a little more company, she stood and offered her hand to the woman. "Thank you. We would love to try it."

The woman exhaled a breath as though she'd been holding it and a smile spread across her lips. "Well, come on. You're more than welcome."

EIGHT

RODERICK

"Why is a pleasure trip to Egypt fit only for a very old person?"

Everyone around the table stared at the young girl as she stood and asked her question. Her face lit up with a smile, and she giggled to herself as the adults glanced around at each other, then back to her. All of them shrugging.

"I don't know, Molly. Why?" her mother asked.

"Because it is a see-NILE thing to do." At the end of her joke, the little girl and the other children, and the adults laughed.

"I have one for you children." Lily leaned toward them, lowering her voice. "Are you all paying attention?" They beamed at her and nodded, completely engrossed in her words. "What do you fill a barrel with to make it lighter?"

Each of the little girls and boys sat back. Some of them cocked their heads to the sides, thinking, while others furrowed their brows, and one even rubbed his fingers on his chin.

"Do you all give up?" Lily asked. And after they all nodded, she straightened her shoulders. "Holes."

The kids started laughing once more and the adults, watching them, laughed even more.

It had been one of the best lunches at the sawmill Roderick had ever seen and one that, as he sat back and watched the men, their wives, and their children having a good time, brought a smile to his face. The morale around the place seemed to lighten, and although it was never a stressful job, having to watch out for accidents made the men cautious. Today, however, for at least the hour they took to eat, a sense of calm seemed to dwell throughout the table.

And it had been all because of Lily starting a joke war with the children.

"I hate to break up the party," Mr. Linwood, Roderick's head sawyer, said. He stood from the table and rubbed his belly before laying his hand on his wife's shoulder. "But us men need to get back to work."

The children all made a saddened noise, and one little girl with pigtail braids looked up at the man with her big, blue, blinking eyes. "But do we have to go?"

"I'm afraid so, little lady. We have to make our quota for the day so we can come home on time."

"Come on, children," Mrs. Linwood said. "Go play near the pond while we gather all the things and let your fathers get back to work." As she stood, so did the rest of the wives, and they began cleaning up and clearing the table.

"I'm going to check on the sawmill and see how everything is running before I take you home," Roderick said to Lily.

"That's all right. Take your time. I will help the wives with the children while you do what you need to do."

She excused herself before he said another word, walking the children down to the pond. An endless slew of questions came at her from all directions as they surrounded her, begging her for more jokes, and he watched them for a moment before turning his attention to the mill.

"Are we in for another smooth afternoon, Mr. Linwood?" he asked.

"Hope so, Mr. Townsend."

The pair of them began circling the boiler, and as Mr. Linwood checked the water levels, Roderick opened the door and threw several pinecones inside, lighting them first before throwing in several logs.

"Looks like it will get hot fast," he said, shutting the door to the boiler.

As the two men waited for the heat to build, Roderick checked the oiler, making sure there was enough oil to mix with the steam while Mr. Linwood checked the governor and the steam chest, draining the water from the cylinders before they opened the valve to raise the revolutions per minute of the engine. As the water dripped from the valve, Mr. Linwood pointed, motioning over toward the pond, and as Roderick followed his finger, he saw Lily playing with the children.

"Where did you find her?" Mr. Linwood asked, twisting the valve. Water poured out in a small stream, and it splattered as it hit the ground, creating a tiny pool in the dirt.

"I don't know. I think she found me."

"Well, aren't you the lucky man, finding her and getting rid of the other one?"

Roderick gave Mr. Linwood a sideways glance. "I beg your pardon?"

"You know, that other girl you brought around a few times. She wasn't friendly. She would never have given the children the time of day." Mr. Linwood pointed toward Lily, who was running around and laughing as the children kicked the ball, trying to keep it away from her.

Roderick couldn't deny the sight of her even made him smile, and he chuckled as she let out a big scream and fell to the ground. The kids surrounded her, and she threw her arms and legs up in the air as if to exaggerate her struggling to keep up with them. They all laughed too, and after one of the older boys helped her up. She gave him a curtsey.

She truly is one of a kind, he thought to himself.

"But that young lady . . ." Mr. Linwood continued. "One thing I know about love and marriage, when you find the right one, you hang on to it. And son, I would hold on to that one for as long as God allowed."

"Thank you for your insight." Roderick inhaled a deep breath, watching Lily for several minutes before turning back to the engine work and helping Mr. Linwood rotate the crankshaft and belt.

Unsure of her thoughts, he only knew his. Or at least he only knew the questions that rolled through his mind. Questions like what she was thinking? Was she unhappy? Was she happy? Did she want to stay in Lone Hollow and marry him? Or had his mother turned her against the idea? He had been trying to read her by the look on her face, the ease in her shoulders when around him, and by her actions, but she wasn't exactly an easy book to read.

In fact, she'd been quite complicated.

Of course, he didn't think of that as a terrible quality to have. He felt it to be something that drew him toward her even more, and he couldn't help but picture them married, living in a house, happy, in love.

Not a terrible picture to imagine, he thought.

With the engine warmed up, Mr. Linwood opened the valve, and the engine chugged faster and faster. The other men began gathering the logs, loading one onto the carriage before another sawyer adjusted the measurements to get the right thickness on the boards.

Mr. Linwood laid his hand on Roderick's shoulder. "We've got this, son. Don't worry. We'll make the quota for today."

"Thank you. I'll let my father know. I would stay, but I must see Miss Prescott home."

"You tell that young lady she's welcome here at the mill

anytime. I might even have her helping me run the sawmill in no time."

"I will. I don't know how she will take to the idea, but I will let her know just the same."

After the two men shook hands, Roderick headed toward the pond, and Roderick and Lily bid a farewell to the children and the wives who had finished cleaning up lunch and had already herded their children away from the mill and toward home.

"Did you have a pleasant time?" he asked her as they strolled down the lane.

"I did. Thank you."

"Mr. Linwood said to tell you that you are welcome any time, and he'd love to show you how to run the mill."

She gave Roderick a wide-eyed gaze for a second, then chuckled. "I don't know about that. But I suppose I could try it."

"He liked you. They all did."

"Well, I had a lot of fun. And the children . . . those families are lucky."

"How many children were at the orphanage with you?"

She shrugged. "It's hard to say. Many arrived, and many left because they were adopted."

"Were there ever any couples interested in adopting you?"

"I think two. For whatever reason, it never worked out with either of them. I never knew why. Miss Whittaker never told me, and I suppose I just figured that if God had meant for them to be mine and for me to be theirs, then it would have happened. He obviously didn't."

"That must have been disappointing."

"It was, and it wasn't. I figured since it didn't work out, there was a reason. Perhaps I would have been unhappy with them."

"I suppose that is one way to look at it." He glanced at her, and for the first time, he studied the lines of her face. Her blue eyes somehow sparkled a little more in the afternoon sunlight, and she had this overwhelming calm about her. It eased his own mind, and he inhaled and exhaled a deep breath.

"You mentioned you don't know who your real father was. Is that true?"

She ducked her chin, and the calm in her just seconds ago faded. Her shoulders tensed, and her brow furrowed.

"Honestly, no. I know who he is, and I know where he is. Well, I know where he was when I was a little girl. My mother left his name and the town he lived in on a scrap of paper with me when she left me at the orphanage."

"What's his name, and where was he?"

"That's the odd part of this entire story . . ." She hesitated, taking in a deep breath. "He is—or was years ago—in Lone Hollow."

Roderick blinked at her. "What's his name?"

She sucked in another breath, letting it out as she whispered the man's name. "Allen Prescott."

'I know Mr. Prescott. He still lives in Lone Hollow. He has a cattle ranch on the outskirts of town. I could take you to see him."

"No!" She stopped dead in her tracks and clutched her throat. "I mean. No, you don't have to do that."

"But don't you want to meet him?"

"It's not about me wishing to meet him. It's about whether he knows about me or wishes to meet me. No, I can't . . . I just can't." She ducked her chin once more and then continued to walk down the lane, passing Roderick. Her pace had doubled into a quick step that he had to trot for a bit to catch up to her.

"My apologies if I said anything to offend you," he said.

"You didn't. However, if we could drop the subject, I would be grateful."

"Consider it dropped."

"Thank you."

She looked as though she was fighting tears, and his gut

twisted with guilt. He hadn't meant to upset her. He only thought to mention knowing the man she knew to be her father and offering to take her to meet him would be a blessing. He'd assumed wrong, however, and he wished he could rewind time to take the comment back.

The last thing he'd wanted to do was make her cry or hurt her feelings.

And unfortunately, he'd done just those things.

"I'm truly sorry for upsetting you," he said.

"It's all right." She gave him a sideways glance before shaking her head as though to shake off her emotions. She sniffed and blinked, then looked up toward the sky. "It was a lovely afternoon. I'm thankful we walked instead of taking the wagon."

"I am too."

"Tomorrow is Sunday, is it not?"

"Yes, it is. Why?"

"Does your family attend church services?"

He nodded. "Would you like to attend?"

"I would. Very much."

"All right, then. We will do just that."

NINE

LILY

"So, remember in *Isaiah 43:18-19:* Forget the former things; do not dwell on the past. See, I am doing a new thing! Now it springs up; do you not perceive it? I am making a way in the wilderness and streams in the wasteland. And it's with this verse I say to you, look for a fresh start in your life. Do not look to the past, for nothing there will do you any good. It is the new day with the Lord that will bring you the ease you need."

Lily sat in the pew, listening to the pastor. It had been what she needed to hear, and yet she feared hearing it because she didn't know what her future held. Would she stay here in Lone Hollow? Or leave and head back to Butte, hoping that the head-mistresses would hire her or allow her to stay until she found a job as a seamstress.

She glanced over at Roderick through the corner of her eye. He sat stoically next to her with his shoulders straight, and his eyes focused on the pastor, as was everyone else around them. Roderick's parents sat on his other side, and although she couldn't see his mother, she could feel the woman's derision even from several feet away. She hadn't been the nicest on the wagon ride into town, nor had she been too pleasant at dinner last night after hearing of Roderick and Lily's afternoon at the sawmill.

Of course, it had been nothing like Lily's first night. However, the under-the-breath remarks and snide comments did little to ease the gut-twisting feeling that plagued Lily when it came to whether or not her intended mother-in-law liked the idea of her for a daughter-in-law.

"And now I ask all of you to look inside your hearts. What is it you want for a fresh start in? What can you shed from your past, leaving it behind, and instead look forward with the Lord? There is no right or wrong answer. There is your answer, and your answer will always be enough in God's eyes."

Out of the corner of Lily's eye, she caught Roderick glancing at her, and the pair turned their chins toward one another but didn't look each other in the eye. Her heart thumped at the reason he acknowledged her. Had the pastor said something to cause his reaction?

A lump formed in her throat, and she tried to swallow it throughout the rest of the sermon and even through the end of the service prayer. It wouldn't budge, and by the time they had stood from the pew and made their way outside after service, it had grown worse.

"Pastor Duncan?" Roderick said as they walked down the stairs. He outstretched his hand, first shaking the pastor's hand, then motioning toward Lily. "I'd like for you to meet Miss Prescott."

"Miss Prescott from Lone Hollow?" The pastor cocked one eyebrow.

"Miss Prescott from Butte," she corrected.

Pastor Duncan gave a tiny nod, then took her hand in his, giving it a slight shake. "Ah. Forgive the confusion. It is a pleasure to meet you, Miss Prescott."

"And I, you."

"So, did you like the sermon today?"

"I did. Very much. It was something I needed to hear."

"Well, that is wonderful to know. It is always my hope to inspire when I'm here."

"And you did today."

The pastor's eyes sparkled slightly as he glanced between Lily and Roderick. "So, Mr. Townsend, are we going to see Miss Prescott more often around Lone Hollow?"

Roderick opened his mouth, but his mother's voice spoke the words.

"We haven't decided upon that yet, Pastor Duncan," she said.

The pastor glanced between the pair once more, then toward Mrs. Townsend. "Well, I know I, for one, certainly hope to see Miss Prescott from now on in my congregation." He gave the couple a wink, and Lily smiled as Mrs. Townsend glared at the pastor and walked off, a slight huff to her breath.

Roderick excused them both as the line of people behind them wishing to talk to the pastor grew, and as they made their way over toward the wagon to leave, he stopped and pointed toward two men, a woman and a young girl with white, blonde hair.

"See those two men?"

"Yes."

"The one on the left is Cullen McCray, and that is his wife, Maggie, and his niece—their adopted daughter—Sadie. The other man is Allen Prescott."

Lily's blood ran cold as she gazed upon the tall man standing next to the horse. His dark hair was slightly greyed in a few spots, like a salt and pepper mix, and dark raven parts of it glistened with a slight blue hue in the sunlight. He was a tall man and the type she could picture her mother falling in love with.

Roderick leaned in, whispering in her ear, "Do you wish to meet him?"

Too stunned to say anything, she shook her head. Her eyes

misted with tears, and she sucked in a breath as she watched him talk and laugh with the married couple. He patted the young girl on the head. She responded to him by wrapping her little arms around his waist, hugging him.

For a moment, she wondered what that would have felt like as a little girl herself. Her father's loving arms wrapped around her, taking away all her fears or worries. She knew she'd missed it, knew she'd longed for it as a little girl, and yet she didn't realize how much until she saw him do it to another girl right before her eyes. It was something she couldn't take.

Not today.

Not after a sermon of starting fresh.

The little girl and him hugging . . . that was the past.

It was all in the past.

"No," she said to Roderick.

Before he opened his mouth to respond, she held up her hand. "I think I'll walk back to the house."

"Walk? It's several miles."

"I don't care." She moved away from him, and although he tried to grab her wrist to stop her, he couldn't get a grip, and she darted down the lane away from the church. He followed her, calling her name a few times until he caught up to her.

"Lily, I didn't mean to upset you. I'm sorry."

"It's not what you did. It's just . . . I'm not ready to meet him, and I don't know if I ever will be."

"I understand, and I shouldn't have asked if you wanted to. It was foolish and unkind—"

"No, it wasn't. To anyone else, it would make sense for you to point him out. Otherwise, I would have wondered every time I saw a man in town if that man was him. Now I know who he is."

Roderick's eyes narrowed. "Do you know what happened between your parents?"

She shook her head. "I know nothing. My mother never

talked about it, and whenever I broached the subject, she changed it. She didn't even tell me the day she left me. She just handed me the piece of paper with his name on it and told me to make my choice."

"That's so odd. You would think she would have told you. At least something."

"It doesn't matter now. He's a stranger . . ." She paused, sucking in another breath as she glanced in the direction where the man still stood with the couple and the young girl. "And he will stay a stranger."

"Are you sure that is what you want?"

"Yes, I'm sure."

"Lone Hollow is a small town. Rumors spread easily."

"You are the only one who knows, so unless you're going to tell anyone—"

"Which I will not." He blinked and stepped toward her as though he was trying to emphasize that he promised not to divulge her secret to anyone. "I swear."

"Then no one should find out. Let him have his life. And I'll have mine." She glanced at the man one last time before turning her attention to Roderick. "Besides, I don't know if I'm staying in Lone Hollow."

Roderick's eyes widened again, and he jerked his head back. "You aren't?"

Her stomach dropped at his reaction. Had he thought differently? "Am I?"

"I don't know why you would leave."

"I know your mother doesn't wish for us to marry, and I was sort of under the impression you shared her feelings. At least you said so the night I arrived. I thought . . . I thought you were just being kind the last few days before your parents sent me home to Butte."

"Well, I can't speak for her." He wiggled his eyebrows, letting out a half-amused snort at his statement as though he thought it absurd even to utter those words. "But I can speak for myself when I say that any reservation I had before your arrival is gone. I would very much like it if you stayed." He paused, swallowing as though he needed a moment to gather courage. "And for us to marry."

It was the second time today that her lungs struggled to find breath, and she brushed her fingertips against her chest. "You would?"

"Yes, I would. That is, if you would have me as your husband. You can say no." He chuckled.

"I don't want to say no. So, yes." Her knees grew weak with her answer. "Yes, I will stay and marry you."

He moved toward her, wrapping his arms around her as he kissed the top of her head. While her body melted into his, her mind screamed about the impropriety of their embrace should anyone see them.

"We shouldn't be seen like this," she said into his chest.

He kissed the top of her head again and whispered. "I don't even care."

TEN

LILY

"It was my grandmother's." Roderick sat next to Lily on the blanket. The gentle afternoon breeze blew through a few of her curls, and she lifted her hand to brush them behind her ear.

Sunlight filtered through the tree branches down on their picnic, and the rays hit the diamond glistening on the gold band. It was a ring, not anything to even compare to her imagination. Far more stunning than she believed a wedding ring could be.

"Do you like it?" he asked.

"Like it? I love it." Her words were more like whispered breaths on her lips, and she brushed her fingertips against her chest. "It's . . . beautiful."

"Well, then it fits the woman who will wear it."

Her cheeks flushed with heat, and she was sure they had turned a bright shade of pink.

"You don't have to say things like that," she said.

"Of course, I do." He chuckled. "And I will for the rest of your life."

"Even when I'm old?"

"Especially when you are old."

He wiggled the ring in his fingers and motioned toward her hand with his chin. "Give me your hand."

She did, and he slipped the band on her left ring finger. A rainbow of color danced from the clear jewel as she moved her hand and gazed down upon it.

"Are you happy?" he asked.

"Such a foolish question, Mr. Townsend." She laughed. "But I shall answer it, anyway."

"And the answer is?"

"Immensely happy."

"That's good to know." He leaned back on his elbow, laying his feet out in front of him as he exhaled a deep breath. "I wish we could stay here all afternoon."

"Why can't we?"

"Mother." He rolled his eyes and fetched a hunk of cheese from the platter sitting near them, shoving it into his mouth. He chewed it and swallowed. "She wants us home for some reason. I don't know why. She wouldn't tell me."

"And did you tell her . . . about us, I mean?"

"Yes. I did." He grabbed a cracker, shoving it in as he did the cheese. After he swallowed that, he blew out a breath, puffing his cheeks for a second.

"It went that well, huh?" Lily knew she wanted to know what happened when Roderick told his mother they were getting married. Yet she also didn't want to know either. She both feared the reaction and wondered how the woman would take the news. She had even spent a few hours out on the porch last night sipping her tea and swinging on the porch swing, waiting to hear screaming coming from the main house.

Instead, all she heard were the crickets and frogs soaking in the coolness of the night.

"It went . . . all right."

"All right, as in? Did she yell?"

"A little. But I don't care. I have made my decision and there is nothing she can do or say to change my mind."

"Nothing?"

"Nothing."

"And it doesn't worry you that your acquaintances in Butte could find out who I am? Could find out that I'm an orphan?"

"I don't care if they do. Why should I? It's not important to me. What is important is the person you are despite your past. I saw you with those children at the picnic at the sawmill. The men and their wives saw too, and they all were impressed. Your past means nothing to me."

"But it does to her." Lily's gut twisted with her words. She had had limited contact with Mrs. Townsend since the day in the barn where the woman had not only pretended to care about Lily but had tricked her onto a horse she never should have ridden in the first place.

"Well, then that is something she's just going to have to get over." He yanked his pocket watch from his pocket, checking the time. A slight growl whispered across his lips. "We should get back to the house."

~

By the time they made it out of the trees and turned the corner up the lane to the house, the dread had built up inside Lily's stomach to the point of her feeling sick. She didn't want to see Mrs. Townsend, didn't want to enter another room where the woman's watchful eye would follow her, mock her, and eventually make her feel as though she were an inch tall. She also didn't want to be at the end of another tongue lashing from the woman, having to dwell in the woman's derision and utmost disgust in Lily's presence.

"Who . . ." Roderick's voice trailed off as he stopped and stood, looking at the house.

"What's the matter?" Lily asked.

He pointed toward the house. "The carriage."

As soon as he mentioned the horse and buggy sitting in front of the house, Lily noticed it. How she had missed it, she didn't know. But she had.

"Do you know who is visiting?"

His lips thinned, and he growled. "Unfortunately, I do."

"Who is it?"

He didn't answer. Instead, he placed his hand on the small of her back, leading her up the stairs, across the porch, and in through the front door, shutting it behind them as she spun in the foyer and asked her question again.

"Follow me."

It was not only his words that rolled like a pit in her stomach, but his tone—a mild annoyance with a hint of dread, and he exhaled a deep breath as he guided her once again, this time to the study.

"Ah. Roderick. There you are. We've been waiting for you." His mother stood as they entered the room. "And you brought Miss Prescott, I see."

"Of course, I did."

Lily moved around him, not only catching sight of his mother standing near the couch, but the two other women sitting in the study with her. All three of them stared at her and she sucked in a breath, wishing she'd stayed hidden behind Roderick.

"Why are they here?" Roderick asked, pointing toward the two women.

"Don't be rude, son. Mrs. Sanderson and Miss Sanderson have come for a visit at my request. They are my guests."

"Which is why I asked why they are here. Why did you send an invitation to them?"

"Because I wanted to see them. You and your father aren't

the only ones who were friends with the family, and I miss their company."

Roderick's shoulders straightened, and tension washed through them.

Lily's heart thumped. She wasn't a fool. She knew who the women were and why Roderick was upset.

"Hello Roderick," the younger of the women said. She stood and smiled at him. Her raven hair was pinned in an elegant updo and while she beamed at Roderick, she glared at Lily with a slight disgust sparkling in her blue eyes. "Aren't you going to introduce me?"

Roderick clenched his teeth, and he glanced at Lily. "Emily, may I introduce you to Miss Lily Prescott," he glanced back at her. "My fiancée."

Emily's eyes widened. "Your fiancée? Your mother hadn't shared that news." The young woman glanced at Mrs. Townsend. "When did this happen?"

"As of yesterday. I asked Miss Prescott to marry me after church."

"Which is yet to be determined, however," Mrs. Townsend said, folding her arms across her chest.

"What is there to determine, Mother? I have asked her, and she has agreed. I have also given her Grandmother's wedding ring." He grabbed Lily's hand, holding it out to show the three women. "We have made it official."

All three women gasped, and while Mrs. Sanderson looked at her daughter, Emily looked at Mrs. Townsend.

"You . . . you failed to mention you were intending on giving her the ring," Mrs. Townsend said.

"What do you mean? I told you last night I intended to give it to her now that she has agreed to marry me." He paused for a moment, glancing between the three of them. "Now, if you will excuse us, I shall see Lily to the guest house. Have a lovely visit,

Mrs. Sanderson, Emily." He began to lead Lily out of the room, but Emily called out, asking him to wait, and he stopped.

"I came not only to see your mother, but to see you. I need to speak to you."

"And what could you possibly have to talk to me about?"

"It's a rather private matter." Her gaze fluttered to Lily. "So, if we could move to another room, just you and me."

Tension washed through Lily's shoulders and although she wanted to shout the word no at the mention of them talking privately in another room, she didn't. She knew an outburst wouldn't be proper, and she didn't need to give Mrs. Townsend another weapon to use against her. No matter how badly she wanted to not care, she did.

"It's all right, Roderick," she said instead, ignoring how her heart thumped against her chest and an imaginary rock rolled around in her stomach. "I will see myself to the guest house. I'm feeling tired from the walk this afternoon, and I should probably rest until dinner."

His brow furrowed as he looked at her. "But I should come with you."

"No, really. Stay and speak with Miss Sanderson. I will see you tonight at dinner."

He gave a weak smile and nodded. A sense of hesitation purred through his movement as he leaned in and kissed her on the cheek. A pain ripped through her heart.

~

RODERICK

*R*oderick watched Lily leave the room. Anger bubbled in his chest and had the women not been present in the room with him, he probably would have punched the wall.

What on earth had he agreed to, he thought. *He was nothing short of a fool.*

"What is it you want?" he asked Emily. His crisp voice snapped.

"You don't need to take a tone with me, Roderick. Even your fiancée doesn't mind if we speak. I don't see what you could be mad about."

He shook his head, blowing out a breath as he motioned toward the door. "After you."

She moved past him, and he followed her, trying to ignore the way she kept glancing over her shoulder as if to make sure he was behind her. She gave him a smile a few times and a wink from the other, prompting him to fix his gaze on the floor.

"Oh, don't tell me you've gone and become a bore." Emily opened the door to the other sitting room.

He followed her inside, and as she sat on the couch, he made his way over to the window across the room. It had a perfect view of the guest house and he watched Lily through the glass as she walked up to the porch, crossed it, and went inside. He didn't want to think about how he longed to be with her instead.

"I have to admit, I was rather shocked to hear of your engagement," Emily said.

"And I was surprised by yours."

"Surprised or jealous?"

He spun to face her. "Jealous? Of what? What could I possibly be jealous of?"

"Of my fiancé. You heard who he is, didn't you?"

"Yes."

"And?"

"And what, Emily?"

"Well, I'm marrying someone of worth."

"Are you saying I'm not?" Heat warmed through his chest as he dropped his voice to a near growl.

She brushed her hand across her chest and batted her eyes. He hated it when she did that—which had been far too often if his memory served him right.

How he ever saw this woman as someone he wanted to marry was beyond him.

Had I been blind, he thought.

"You know I would never say anything. However, I'm only repeating what your mother told me."

"Which was?"

"That she's a nobody. An orphan and someone your father sent for, to marry you." A hint of amusement whispered through her words. "What were the words she used . . . mail-order bride."

"She's not a nobody, Emily, and the fact that you would even say as much . . ."

"Does what?"

He shook his head, biting his tongue. He wanted to be rude but stopped himself. He would be better than the malicious being sitting on the couch across the room from him.

"She's an amazing young woman," he said instead. "And so what if my father sent for her? If that is how two people are to meet and come to fall in love, then it should hold no shame."

"Fall in love?"

"Yes, fall in love. I have fallen for her, and she has fallen for me." He paused, narrowing his gaze at Emily. "She sees me as more than just money and a horrible scar she couldn't live with."

As soon as the words left his lips, there was a part of him that regretted them. He hadn't wanted to bring up his scar, hadn't wanted her to know how her dismissal of him because of his appearance had wounded him all those months ago.

Emily inhaled a deep breath, and she stood from the couch, making her way over to him. "I don't wish to fight anymore, Roderick. I didn't come here for that."

"Then what did you come here for?"

"I came to tell you that . . . while I love Stewart . . . I . . . I miss you. The Dowrey's are wealthy, and they will give me a lovely life as their daughter-in-law, but . . . but Stewart. He isn't you. I miss you and I think I made a mistake in breaking off our courtship."

Emily's words hit him like an out-of-control horse, barreling down a trail and hitting anything in its path. Months ago, he would have loved to have heard them, but now? Now he only wished she hadn't said them. He didn't want Emily Sanderson anymore. He only wanted one woman—Lily Prescott.

"Do you miss me?" she asked, inching closer to him. He wanted to back away from her, but something stopped him. He was determined not to allow her to dictate anything he did, thought, or said anymore.

"No. I don't."

"Oh, don't lie to me. You know you miss me." She finally reached him, and she placed her hands on his chest. Her touch was light, tender. The same touch he'd known since they were children and throughout their courtship.

He hated it.

"I honestly don't, Emily. Now, if you will excuse me, I must see to my fiancée. I shall see you at your engagement party. I wish you and Mr. Dowery all the happiness you can give each other." He backed away from her, cocking his head to the side. "Which, given how you are so quick to cast him aside, doesn't seem like much."

He moved toward the door.

"Don't do something you will regret, Roderick Townsend," Emily called after him.

"The only thing I regret is ever loving you."

He left the room, slamming the door behind him.

ELEVEN

LILY

*L*ily had thought of nothing else but the visit by Emily and her mother over the last few days. Although she had wanted to ask Roderick what they said in their private conversation, she never asked, and he never offered the information. She didn't know why, but she figured he had his reasons and was entitled to them.

Or at least that was what she believed.

Perhaps some would say otherwise. She didn't know.

"I'm not looking forward to tonight," he whispered as they followed his parents up the stairs toward the front door of the Sanderson's Estate.

It'd been a few weeks since Lily had been in Butte again, and while she had looked forward to seeing the familiar city, there was also a dark cloud that had loomed over her thoughts of the visit.

They weren't there to see Miss Whittaker or the orphanage. They were there to attend the engagement party of Emily Sanderson and Stewart Dowery.

"I can't say that I blame you. I'm not exactly looking forward to it either." She glanced over at him as he lifted his hand to the opposite side of her head, drawing her closer to him so he could kiss her on the head.

"I'm sorry you have to attend what, I'm sure, will not be a pleasant evening."

She shrugged. "I would rather be here with you than be alone at the house in Lone Hollow."

"Agreed. I would rather you here with me than there alone, too."

They both exchanged looks, and he smiled at her, giving her a wink.

The inside of the manor was lit up nearly floor to ceiling with not only light from the crystal chandelier and wall sconces but from candles that were lit and placed on all the shelves around the foyer. The candlelight bounced off the cream-colored walls and dark hardwood floors, illuminating the entire place with a soft glow. Lily sucked in a breath as she glanced around the room. Every inch of the house downstairs mimicked an indoor flower garden with bouquets of gardenias, roses, white carnations, and baby's breath, with garlands wrapped around each staircase railing and arched over every doorway.

Roderick leaned in, whispering in her ear. "One thing to know about Mr. Sanderson . . . he's always one to spare no expense when it comes to hosting a party. And by the looks of it, he certainly didn't disappoint tonight."

"I think it's beautiful," Lily said.

"It smells like a perfume bottle."

"Complaining already?" She snorted a laugh as she gave him a sideways glance.

"Already? My darling, I was complaining about this party from the moment I heard we were going to have to attend."

Lily laughed again as he led her through the crowd after his parents.

A nervous flutter whispered through her chest and stomach, and she held every other breath until her lungs begged her just to breathe. Roderick kept his hand on the small of her back, and she pressed into his fingers more and more as they passed through the crowd of people, who all smiled and nodded in their direction.

Of course, she knew none of them. However, while a part of her considered this a good thing, there was also a part of her that wondered if it was. She didn't know the lies Mrs. Townsend had planned to tell everyone, and she didn't want to make a mistake.

"Mr. and Mrs. Sanderson!" Mr. Townsend outstretched his hand as he approached two couples. After shaking the first man's hand, he took the woman's hand in his and kissed the back of it before turning to the other couple. "And Mr. and Mrs. Dowery, it is a pleasure to see you again." He mimicked the greeting to the other couple—shaking Mr. Dowery's hand first before kissing the back of Mrs. Dowery's gloved hand. "I'd like to present my wife, Caroline, and my son, Roderick, and his newly welcomed fiancée, Miss Prescott."

While the four smiled and acknowledged Mrs. Townsend, they passed her by within seconds, focusing on Lily.

Lily's heart thumped as she nodded and shook their hands.

"It's a pleasure to meet you, my dear," Mrs. Dowery said.

"Yes, I have to agree. It is," Mrs. Sanderson added as she looked down at Lily's shoes, letting her gaze trace up to her body and back to her face. "And may I say congratulations on your engagement, Roderick? We had hoped you would find happiness as Emily has found it after . . . well, after you two decided not to get married."

Roderick smiled, his eyes narrowed slightly, and his fingers pressed into Lily's back, scraping along the buttons of her dress. She didn't know what it meant, though. Was it his way of conveying to her how much he loathed this conversation? Or was he unhappy with how things were after speaking to Emily that day after he gave Lily the ring?

"Yes," he said. "It is a wonderful thing when something amazing can come from a less than pleasurable moment." He paused for a moment, moving Lily over to his other side. "If you will please excuse us, I must see that my fiancée has some refreshment after our long journey from Lone Hollow."

They all nodded, but before Lily and Roderick could get too far, Mrs. Townsend stopped them, grabbing his arm.

"Roderick, dear, I wonder if I may borrow Lily before you take her away. I wish to introduce her to some ladies first."

A lump formed in Lily's throat. She didn't want to be alone with this woman any more than she wanted to poke her own eyes out with a fork. And she certainly didn't wish to meet any of Mrs. Townsend's friends.

"Does it have to be now, Mother?" Roderick asked.

"Yes, I'm afraid it does."

Roderick hesitated but then nodded, leaning into Lily's ear to whisper, "I shall wait for you over by the refreshments table."

Unable to speak with the knot in her throat, she nodded and followed Mrs. Townsend off through the crowd, trying her best to hold on to the feeling of his hand on her back. The farther she weaved through the people, however, the more his touch vanished, and she closed her eyes for a moment to stop the dread building in her chest.

"Ah, right in here, I think will be fine."

"In where?"

Mrs. Townsend pointed toward a room. The door was slightly ajar, and as Lily stepped through it, Mrs. Townsend followed.

No one else was in there.

"Who is it you wished for me to meet?" Lily asked. A part of her didn't want to know the answer, but she asked anyway.

"Huh? Oh, no one. I just wanted to get a moment with you alone to tell you something I think you should know."

"And what is that?"

"What happened between Roderick and Emily the other day when she visited. I don't know if he's told you or not, but given the fact that you are still here, I doubt it."

"And what is that supposed to mean?"

"It means I don't think he told you, or if he did, I don't think he told you the truth."

"And what is the truth?"

Mrs. Townsend folded her arms across her chest. "The truth is they both still share feelings for one another, and they both regret ending their courtship."

"If that is true, then why are we here for Emily's engagement party?"

"The party had already been planned, and the Sanderson's and the Dowery's didn't want to face the embarrassment of calling it off. So, they went along with the party. Then afterward, like next week, they will announce that Emily and Stewart are no longer engaged. At that time, Emily and Roderick will be free to announce their engagement."

"And how . . . how am I supposed to trust what you are telling me is the truth?"

Mrs. Townsend dropped her gaze to the floor and stepped closer to Lily as she reached out and laid her hand on Lily's shoulder. "I understand. I haven't given you much reason to trust me, and I am sorry for that. It's true I've been against your courtship since you arrived. But it was only because I knew Roderick belonged with Emily, and I didn't want you—an innocent girl—to get wrapped up in a mess that you shouldn't be wrapped up in. I knew how this would end, and I didn't want you to have to face a broken heart. I was trying to do you a favor, even if I did it poorly. I hope you can forgive my . . . not so friendly behavior."

Although Lily didn't want to believe the woman, she couldn't help but feel that perhaps she was speaking the truth. Why else hadn't Roderick mentioned his conversation with

Emily to her? If he had, she would have left, and then he would have arrived at Emily's engagement party alone. Of course, it made perfect sense. The only two people who would face the embarrassment of this backlash were Stewart and her.

Lily stepped away from Mrs. Townsend as she stared at the floor.

"I do apologize for my husband getting you into such a mess, and if there is anything I can help you with—money to help you get back to your orphanage . . . or anywhere else you would like to go. I'd be more than happy to give you what you need."

"I don't need your money."

"I'm sorry that I didn't have time to tell you all of this before we left Lone Hollow."

"It's all right. I think . . . I think I need to leave."

"That's probably for the best, dear before Roderick introduces you to even more people. You know how rumors have such a way of spreading around and, well, although I don't suppose you will ever socialize with anyone here after tonight . . . I just wouldn't want you to face any more embarrassment."

"No, you're right. It was nice meeting you. I'll see myself out."

Lily didn't want to spend another minute in Mrs. Townsend's company. She also didn't want to spend another minute, not only in the room but in the Sanderson's manor. She didn't even know if she wished to say goodbye to Roderick, but as she weaved through the crowd, she spied him standing near the refreshment table, speaking to none other than Emily herself.

Lily's anger flared, and she approached them with heat warming through her chest.

"Goodbye, Roderick," she said.

His brow furrowed, and he set his glass of punch down on the table before moving in front of her. "What do you mean goodbye?"

"I know what the plan is, and I will not give you the satisfaction of humiliating me. Even if I know no one here and probably will never see anyone again. It's just . . . I can't take it."

"What are you talking about?"

"Your mother informed me of your and Emily's plan."

"What plan?"

Emily stepped toward them, brushing her fingers against her cheek. "You know, Roderick. The plan." She wiggled her eyebrows.

Lily's gut twisted. She had wanted to think that it had been another lie Mrs. Townsend told, however, Emily's reaction . . .

How could it not be true, she thought.

"I don't know what you're talking about?" Roderick shook his head, narrowing his gaze at the raven-haired girl for a moment before glancing back to Lily. "Whatever it is my mother told you, it isn't true."

"But it is," Emily said. "All of it is."

Roderick closed his eyes for a moment. His jaw clenched, and he reached out, trying to lay his hand on Lily's shoulder. She moved.

"Lily, please. Don't."

"Don't what? Leave? Why should I stay?"

"Because I do not know what you're talking about."

"Let her go, Roderick," Emily said. "It's better for her to leave. She's only going to face more talk if she stays, and you wouldn't want that for her, would you?"

"Emily, be quiet. I don't want to hear another word from you."

"But you obviously will not tell her the truth. Honestly, I don't even know why you brought her here after what we agreed upon. I suppose it was to make you look good. Have someone on your arm; someone people can know that you dismissed after I break it off with Stewart so we can be together."

"What?" He gaped at her. His shoulders straightened, and although he'd kept his attention on Lily for the last few minutes, he moved around her, approaching Emily. "What did you say?"

Lily didn't wait around for Emily's answer, and she darted for the door, rushing through it as another couple was trying to enter. She shoved them aside, not caring about their shock or the words the husband shouted at her regarding her rudeness as she dashed across the porch, down the stairs, and out onto the cobble path down the street.

Her eyes filled with tears that streamed down her cheeks, and although she heard Roderick calling after her, she didn't look back. There was only one place she longed to be—the orphanage—and it was across town. She'd run all the way there if she had to.

And she did.

TWELVE

RODERICK

"*Would* someone care to explain to me what just happened?" Roderick slammed the door behind them and turned to face his parents, Emily, and her parents. Still out of breath from trying to run after Lily, his lungs heaved, and droplets of sweat beaded along his forehead.

"What are you talking about, son?" his father asked.

"I'm talking about the fact that Lily is gone, and it's because these two," he pointed toward Emily and his mother, "told her of some plan that I know nothing about."

"What plan?"

"I don't know. But apparently, it has something to do with Emily breaking it off with Stewart and me breaking it off with Lily so we can be together again."

"You did what?" Mr. Sanderson stepped forward, staring at his wife and daughter. "What on earth were you thinking?" His voice raised into a shout.

"I would not go through with it, Daddy," Emily said. She folded her arms across her chest and stuck her bottom lip out. "I only wanted to get rid of the girl."

"I beg your pardon?" Caroline moved around her husband,

marching up to Emily. "How dare you lie to me. You told me you wanted him back."

"Well, I did. But then Mama reminded me of what I'd be giving up. The Dowery's . . . well, they are rather wealthy people, and I would have more opportunities if I were their daughter-in-law than I would if I was yours." Emily rolled her eyes toward the ceiling, not meeting his mother's hard stare. She kept her eyes focused on the wall across the room as though she was trying to do everything in her power not to make eye contact with anyone.

"And you?" His mother turned to Mrs. Sanderson. "You had a part to play in this. What happened to all those things you told me that day you visited?"

"I changed my mind." Mrs. Sanderson cocked her head to the side. "It is in my best interest, as well as my daughter's best interest, for her to marry Stewart."

"How dare both of you do this me." His mother threw her hands up in the air, and as she stepped toward them, Mr. Sanderson moved between her and them, blocking her way.

"I think my wife and daughter have made themselves quite clear. The subject should be dropped from now on."

"I would have to agree," his father said.

Roderick's parents exchanged heated glances, and as his father waved off his mother, she turned her hardness toward Mr. and Mrs. Sanderson. Roderick half expected her to say something, furthering her argument, but she remained silent.

"Now," Mr. Sanderson continued. "If you will excuse us. This is obviously a family matter, and we have a house full of guests to entertain. Not to mention, I'm sure Stewart is wondering where his fiancée is, and I wouldn't wish for him to know anything that happened here tonight." He pointed toward Roderick's mother. "Have I made myself clear?"

"Clear on what?" she said, her voice crisp.

"You will not speak a word of this to Stewart or Mr. and Mrs. Dowery. Am I clear?"

"Yes, yes, of course." Roderick's mother rolled her eyes, waving her hand.

Roderick stood in silence as the three Sandersons left the room. He paced a few times and then stopped, rubbing his forehead with his hand. A slight growl rumbled through his chest. He didn't know where he wanted to begin, but he knew he couldn't say nothing.

"I just . . . I want to know what you were thinking," he said to his mother.

"I was only thinking of your happiness."

"My happiness?" He blinked at her, a slight snorted laugh whispered through his nose. "So, did it occur to you at all that I could have found happiness in Lily?"

"She isn't meant to be yours, Roderick. If she were, your father wouldn't have had to send for her. She wouldn't be a mail-order bride." Her tone changed with the last of her words.

"And what is wrong with that?"

"I'm curious to know myself, considering." His father let out a deep sigh and shoved his hands into his pockets.

Roderick glanced between his parents. "What do you mean?" he asked his father.

"Zachary, I don't think now is the time to get into this." His mother shot her husband a glare.

"Why not? I think the boy is entitled to know the truth."

"The truth about what?" Roderick asked. His eyes narrowed.

"About how I met your mother and our marriage."

"Now is not the time." His mother threw up her hands and paced, just as her son had. Only unlike him, she didn't stop after just a few minutes.

"I don't understand." Roderick watched her for a moment, then turned his attention to his father. "How did you two meet?"

"She was a mail-order bride."

Roderick's mouth gaped open, and the air was kicked from his lungs. "But . . . but . . . why are you so against her? You acted as though she was no better than the manure on my shoe because she was a mail-order bride. And here I find out you were one too. I don't understand."

"It's because I wanted better for you. Better than a marriage built on force rather than love." She finally stopped pacing and stood facing the two men. "I had to marry your father. I didn't want to. And while I can't say that love didn't blossom, there . . . it was all started with the pressure of our families."

"You act as though you didn't want to marry me," his father said.

"I didn't. I was courting Billy Thomas."

"Billy Thomas is a half-wit and has no direction in life. Your parents knew it, and that is why they agreed to our marriage. He works down at the lumberyard in Butte, making not even a tenth of the money I support you with."

"I know. But that doesn't mean I didn't have feelings for him when I was a girl."

"And do you still have feelings for him?"

"Certainly not." Her brow furrowed, and she deepened her voice in annoyance. "But that doesn't mean I wasn't heartbroken at the time. And I didn't want my son to go through the same."

"Well, congratulations, Mother, you've succeeded. Because that's exactly what I'm going through."

"What do you mean?"

"I loved her."

"Emily?"

"No, not Emily. I loved Lily, and now because of you, she's gone."

~

LILY

*B*y the time Lily reached the orphanage, she trembled not only from the cold but from her sobs. While this place still felt like home, she didn't know how she felt about seeing it again. She knew she couldn't stay, and yet, with nowhere else to go, she had no choice.

She had to take the risk.

She trudged up the stairs, and her bare feet inched across the wood. She'd taken her shoes off miles ago, as the pain they caused had made her cry even more. She knocked on the door and waited.

The sound of footsteps thumped on the other side, and the door opened a crack. A woman's voice came from the darkness behind it.

"How may I help you?" the woman said.

"Miss Whittaker? It's Lily . . . Lily Prescott. May I come in?"

The door opened more, and Miss Whittaker stepped into the light of the porch. "Lily? What are you doing here?" She looked down at Lily's feet. "And where are your shoes?"

Lily lifted her arm, holding her shoes in one hand. The laces had been hooked around her finger, and the shoes swayed with her movement. "May I come in?" she asked again.

"Well, of course, you may." Miss Whittaker waved Lily inside, shutting the door behind her. "Come on inside the sitting room. I have a fire going, and I can make you some tea while you sit and warm up."

"I'm not cold."

"Well, it will still do you some good to sit by a fire and drink a cup of tea." The woman guided Lily into the sitting room. A warm light glowed from the hearth, and the warmth washed over Lily's skin. The hairs on her arms stood. She sat down on the couch, watching the flames flicker around the log as Miss Whittaker left to fetch the tea. More tears filled her eyes and streamed down her cheeks, and she sniffed as she wiped them away. She always hated crying in front of people.

"All right," Miss Whittaker said, coming back into the sitting room. She held a tray in her hands, and she set it down on the coffee table in front of the couch. "If I remember correctly, it's cream and sugar, right?"

"Yes," Lily whispered, offering the woman a smile.

Miss Whittaker nodded, pouring some cream in a cup before adding the sugar and pouring in the tea. Steam rose from the cup, and she handed it to Lily, who took it and held it in the palm of one hand. Her finger of the other hooked through the ring of the handle.

"Are you warming up?" Miss Whittaker asked.

Lily nodded. "I didn't think I was chilled, but I suppose I was, after all. Thank you."

"I didn't expect you ever to come back. But it's nice to see you. You look all dressed up. Are you in town for a party?"

Miss Whittaker sat down on the couch across from the other, folding her hands in her lap as she stared at Lily. Her face bordered concerned with a hint of caution, as though she wanted to inquire as to why Lily was there but also didn't want to upset the girl any more than she already was.

"Something like that." Lily dropped her gaze to the teacup in her lap. "I was attending the engagement party for a young woman to Mr. Stewart Dowery."

"Of the banks?"

"Yes."

"Oh." Miss Whittaker blinked. Her word was more of a breath than a word. "Fancy. That would explain the dress. You look beautiful, by the way. Did the young Mr. Townsend go with you? To the party, I mean?"

Lily nodded. "Yes, he did. But I left him there."

"Left him?" Miss Whittaker cocked her head to the side. "What do you mean, dear?"

Lily shrugged. "I don't know if I wish to discuss it. Would it be all right if I stayed here tonight?"

"Well, of course, it would. You are always welcome. I will just tell the other headmistresses that you are visiting . . . should they take issue with it."

"Thank you. I'm quite tired. I walked a long way. If I may, can I go upstairs and rest in my old bed?"

"Of course. Let me make sure to get you another blanket."

Lily followed the woman to the cupboard in the hallway, where Miss Whittaker stopped and opened the door, fetching a blanket from one shelf.

"If you need anything else . . ."

"I know," Lily said, taking the blanket. "I will let you know."

"Are you sure you don't wish to talk about what happened tonight and why you are here?"

"No, Miss Whittaker. I'd rather not. At least for right now."

'Well, all right, dear. If you change your mind, I will be in the sitting room reading for at least another hour."

"I know. I remember your nightly routine."

Before the woman could say another word, Lily headed upstairs, clutching the blanket tight to her chest. Although in the first week of leaving the orphanage, it had been the one place she had longed to go back to, that feeling had since vanished after Roderick had proposed, and coming back now only brought her more heartbreak.

Yet again, she had a chance for a home. A proper home with a family—even if that family was her and a husband.

And now, yet again, it had been ripped away from her.

THIRTEEN

RODERICK

*I*t had been weeks since the party, and Roderick had made many attempts to find Lily and had even written to Mr. Benson, the marriage broker, hoping he would know how to get in touch with her. So far, nothing had worked. It was as though she had vanished off the earth, leaving behind a hole in his heart as the only clue she'd even existed.

He tried to stop thinking about her, at least during the day at the sawmill, but most of the time, his efforts were nothing but the wayward notions of a fool trying to do something impossible. She invaded his thoughts from dawn to dusk, and everything around him only reminded him of her more.

It was the worst feeling of loss he'd ever had—even more so than when Emily told him she was leaving, and it was over.

Emily.

The thought of that woman now only simmered his blood. He blamed her. Blamed her for everything. He didn't know what she was thinking. Had she missed him? Was she going to leave Stewart Dowery, one of the wealthiest men in Butte, for him? Somehow Roderick doubted it. While it wasn't easy thinking of himself as a lesser man, he also couldn't deny the truth. Sure, he had his own money, but it wasn't like the Dowery's money. And knowing Emily . . . there was no way she would have walked away from that opportunity. So why had she done it? Why had she gone along with the stories, with the lies? Was it just because she didn't want him with anyone? Although he had wanted to know, he supposed, in the end, he didn't. It didn't matter. All that mattered was he blamed her.

And he blamed his mother. He had had a gut feeling that night to not go to Emily's engagement party, but foolishly he'd ignored it and went anyway, taking Lily along where she had to face the attack from the wolves. How he had put her in that position . . . it was something he didn't know if he'd ever forgive himself for.

He also didn't know if he'd ever forgive his mother.

His mother.

He hadn't seen her since the party, either. After the admissions, after her secrets had finally come to light, she and his father agreed to stay in Butte at their house in the city. It had been the concession his father allowed, leaving Roderick the house, sawmill, and the family business while his parents remained in Butte, handling part of the business dealings that Roderick never wanted to handle again—namely socializing with the likes of their high society acquaintances, attending parties, and brokering new business deals.

"It's time for you to take over, son," his father had said. "Everything is yours."

His.

It was a glorious thought and yet a painful one, too.

He'd been hoping to share it all with Lily.

And now, he shared it with no one.

He stood near the mill engine, watching the bright red balls on the governor spin, opening and closing as the engine turned. A few times, his mind would wander, and his gaze would turn fuzzy. He knew work was good for a man in his state, but he also couldn't help but long for home. Why? He didn't know. He was just as lonely there and without the distraction of the other men and work; it was almost worse.

"You doing all right, Mr. Townsend?" Mr. Linwood asked.

Roderick shook his head, focusing his gaze on the old man. "Of course. I want to get all those logs cut today if we can." He pointed toward a pile that deep down he knew was probably too large to finish in one day.

Mr. Linwood hesitated, giving him an odd sideways glance as he chewed on a long piece of straw hanging from his mouth.

"Or at least as much of it as we can," Roderick corrected himself, trying to give Mr. Linwood an encouraging smile. "Mr. and the new Mrs. McCray are trying to rebuild their barn, and he put in a rather large order I would like to fill as soon as we can."

"You're the boss. We'll try to get to as much of it as we can, then we'll finish it tomorrow."

"Sounds good."

Roderick moved around the engine and over toward the blade and carriage. He watched the other two men load a log, setting the thickness measurement before slowly inching it toward the blade. He had once feared the spinning piece of metal. Having been caught in it, he knew what it felt like and the damage it could do. He'd been one of the lucky ones. Most men who get tangled with a spinning blade don't live to tell the tale. But he had, and he watched as it sliced through the log, sending chunks of bark and flakes of sawdust in all directions with a sense of wonder and trepidation.

"Hans!" Mr. Linwood shouted behind Roderick. "Hans, you fool!" Roderick spun as Mr. Linwood darted from the engine to the boiler. "I told you to check the water to make sure the crown sheet was protected!"

A rock sank in Roderick's stomach as he dashed over to the boiler. Steam poured out of the door.

"Get back, Mr. Townsend; this thing could blow!" The old man shoved Roderick, but he advanced anyway. He couldn't lose the boiler. Losing it would set him back weeks, if not months, in work. This couldn't be how he handled the business in just the few weeks after his father handed everything over. Not to mention, men in town depended on the sawmill. They depended on him to get them the wood to build their homes, barns, and businesses.

He skirted around Mr. Linwood, making his way over to the boiler. More steam poured out, and he could feel the heat from the outside of the metal. He checked the water levels. Zero. Zilch. It had no water left. The crown sheet would heat within seconds.

Before he could spin to run, the boiler blew, sending flames, hot burning chunks of wood and ash, and pieces of metal flying.

~

LILY

"*L*ily! Lily, where are you?" Mrs. Meyer called out from across the dress shop.

Lily was down on the floor, tending to the loose nail in one of the boards, and in a mid stroke, she held the hammer over her head as she glanced up. "I'm over here, Mrs. Meyer." She sat on her heels, waving her hand.

"Goodness, child." The woman brushed her hand against her chest. "You scared me. What on earth are you doing on the floor?"

"I'm trying to fix that nail you wished for me to fix."

"Oh. Well, never mind that nail. Get up and get to the back. We have an important woman coming in today to get fitted for a custom wedding dress."

In the few weeks since Lily left the party and Roderick

Townsend, she'd managed to get a job at a dress shop. Miss Whittaker had known Mrs. Meyers for years and, as a favor amongst friend and friend, Lily had started at a handsome wage, allowing her to save quite a bit of money in just a short time. Which, since the headmistresses at the orphanage had only given her a month's stay, was also a blessing.

And one she thanked God for every day in her prayers.

"I need all the fitting supplies from the back and organized near the mirrors." The woman clapped her hands. "I want everything in order before the young lady, her mother, and future mother-in-law arrive. Do you understand me?"

"Yes, Mrs. Meyer." Lily wasted no time darting into the back storage room. She gathered all the measuring tapes, the pin holders, and even some fabrics she'd seen Mrs. Meyer use as a pattern when creating a dress. Her heart thumped with her work, and she set everything out and in order, trying to ignore how her hands trembled.

Although Mrs. Meyer was a calm woman, not at all demanding, there were times she would become a bit of an arduous person—usually when she had a deadline, or she wanted to impress a customer. It was understandable to Lily, and she always made sure she worked extra hard to help the woman as best she could.

The bell above the door chimed, and Lily heard Mrs. Meyer welcome the expectant customers just as she finished up. She tried to dart to the storage room, where Mrs. Meyer often sent her when she was helping someone but stopped as she rounded the corner and came face to face with none other than Emily Sanderson.

"You?" Emily scoffed. "What are you doing here?"

Mrs. Meyer halted in her tracks, as well as Mrs. Sanderson and Mrs. Dowery.

"My apologies, Miss Sanderson," Lily's boss said, a slight chuckle whispered through her words. "My assistant was just headed to the stockroom. If you wish to follow me over to the mirror, we shall start planning the wedding dress of the season. Isn't that what you wanted, Mrs. Sanderson?" she asked Emily's mother.

"Never mind the dress. What is she doing here?" Emily pointed toward Lily.

"I work here. I'm Mrs. Meyer's assistant."

Emily turned toward Mrs. Meyer. "Are you going to allow her to touch my wedding dress?"

"No, Miss Sanderson, of course not. I will be the only one touching the dress."

"And the material?"

"And the material. I will make sure she doesn't touch one stitch."

Emily glanced between Mrs. Meyer and Lily with one eyebrow cocked.

"What does it matter, Emily?" Her mother asked. "Let's just get on with the fitting. You have a luncheon with Stewart in a few hours, and you don't want to keep your fiancé waiting."

"Fiancé?" Although Lily knew she should have bitten her tongue, she couldn't help herself, and seeing Mrs. Meyer whip her head toward her assistant in horror; Lily immediately regretted speaking at all.

"You didn't think I would give Stewart Dowery up for the likes of Roderick Townsend, do you? Not only is Stewart worth ten times the money, but he also doesn't have that ghastly scar on his face." Emily rolled her eyes. "Lord, I worried for days and days about how I was going to live with the sight of that scar for the rest of my life. And what to tell people?"

"If you didn't want Roderick to marry you . . . then why did you say there was a plan at the party?"

"Oh, I don't know. I was quite bored that night. And everyone was non-stop talking about who the woman was with Roderick Townsend. Of course, after the two of you left, we all had quite fun talking about how his father paid you to marry him."

"He never paid me."

"Whatever. Anyway, everyone laughed, and it made the evening so much more fun. You really should have been there."

Lily's blood boiled in her veins. She glanced at Mrs. Meyer, who, with wide eyes, shook her head, then at Mrs. Sanderson and Mrs. Dowery, who both had their gazes trained on the room around them as they both pretended the scene before them wasn't happening.

Lily opened her mouth but closed it before she said a word. So many things sat on the tip of her tongue, but along with them came the responsible part of her that screamed for her to stay quiet. Not only did she need the job, but she didn't want to embarrass Miss Whittaker.

She dropped her gaze to the floor. Her shoulders hunched. "I will be in the stockroom should you need anything, Mrs. Meyer." Without taking her gaze from the hardwood, she walked away from the four women.

"He was telling you the truth, by the way," Emily said to her as she passed.

Lily glanced over her shoulder. "I beg your pardon?"

"He was telling you the truth at the party. He knew nothing of the plan. Not that there was one, as I said. He was telling you the truth. So, I suppose . . . you can have him for all I care. I was bored with Roderick long ago, and I've got much more important matters on my mind."

"Of course, you do."

"What did you say?" Emily's eyes narrowed.

"I just meant that now you have ruined Roderick's life and my life . . . I suppose you will turn your attention to ruining Stewart's life. I'm quite shocked at you, Mrs. Dowery. Allowing such a union for your son. I would think you would want better for him."

"Why you little—" Emily stepped forward, but so did Mrs. Meyer, and the older lady blocked, the younger, stopping the latter in her tracks. Anger flared in Emily's eyes, and she pointed at Lily as a warning.

"Lily, leave my shop at once," Mrs. Meyer said. "You are no longer employed here."

"I understand, Mrs. Meyer, and I'm sorry for my disrespect. I shall come by later for the rest of my pay."

"No need. I will see that it gets to Miss Whittaker before the day is out."

"Thank you."

Lily's eyes misted with tears as she headed for the door and shoved it open. She was right back to where she started from. No job. No place to go. And now, all she could think of was the guilt she had for not believing—and not listening to—Roderick.

Oh, how he must hate me, she thought.

FOURTEEN

LILY

*L*ily didn't know how to tell Miss Whittaker about what happened at the dress shop. Her gut twisted the entire walk home, and as she entered the orphanage and made her way into the kitchen, she felt as though she could wretch at any second.

"Miss Whittaker?"

"Come here, child. Sit down." Miss Whittaker was as pale white as a ghost, and she barely looked Lily in the eyes as she motioned her to take a seat in one of the chairs. The woman blew out a breath.

Had Mrs. Meyer somehow gotten word to Miss Whittaker before Lily could make it home? There wasn't any chance she could know about what happened. Is there?

"Have you seen the newspapers this morning?" Miss Whittaker asked.

"Newspapers?"

"Yes, have you seen the headlines in the newspapers this morning?"

"Oh. No, I haven't. But listen, I have to tell you—"

"So, you don't know?"

"Know what?"

Lily's heart thumped. Is that how she knew what had happened? Had there been an article in the newspaper about Emily Sanderson, fiancé to Stewart Dowery, planning on visiting the dress shop this afternoon for her first wedding dress fitting? Lily wanted to roll her eyes but fought the urge.

Miss Whittaker grabbed the paper from behind the basket of apples then made her way over to the table. She glanced down at Lily and, with a deep inhaled breath, handed her the rolled-up news.

Lily unfolded it and opened it to the front page, tracing the different articles. "I don't know what you're referring to. Which article is it you are wondering if I saw?"

"That one," Miss Whittaker pointed toward the bottom of the page.

Lily glanced down, reading the headline . . .

BOILER EXPLOSION AT A SAWMILL IN LONE HOLLOW: THREE MEN KILLED, THREE MORE INJURED

Her heart thumped. "Does it give the names of the dead and wounded?" she asked the old woman, not knowing if she desired to read the article.

Miss Whittaker shook her head. "It says they are still trying to determine the men's identities. The three that survived . . . they are burned, and each of them is in a coma."

Lily let the newspaper fall from her fingers, and it hit the table. The pages scattered from one another, falling all over the wood. "I've got to go. I need to catch the stagecoach to Lone Hollow."

"Here," Miss Whittaker dug her hand into her pocket. "Take this." She handed Lily some money.

"I don't need it. I have plenty."

"Well, then here, take these." She ran to the cupboard and

yanked the bottles of linseed and limewater from the shelves, handing them to Lily. "You never know if you will need them."

"I'm sure the doctors will have done what they can for them."

"I know. But you never know."

Lily wanted to refuse again, but she smiled and hugged the woman. "Thank you for all your help. I shall write to you when I get there to let you know what is going on."

"Then I shall await your letter, and I will let Mrs. Meyer know you will not be in. However, I'm afraid she might not take the news too kindly."

"I wouldn't think she would, given she fired me today."

"What happened?"

"Emily Sanderson came in this afternoon for a wedding dress fitting, and I'm afraid I opened my mouth."

"Well, I'm sure whatever you said was warranted. I shall have a word with Mrs. Meyer about it. Let her know how I feel about the subject. Trust me. She's going to regret letting you go before I'm done with her." Miss Whittaker gave Lily a wink, then shooed her from the kitchen with the orders to hurry and write to her when Lily was settled.

~

*L*ily banged on the front door of the Townsend's house. She cared not for the lateness of the hour or if it would bother Mr. Townsend or Mrs. Townsend. Not at all. She had to know if Roderick was dead or one of the men who were alive but in a coma.

No one opened the door, and there wasn't even a sound of footsteps coming to the door.

She knocked again, and still nothing.

Moving over to the window, she gazed inside the glass. A few lights were on in the foyer and up the staircase to the second floor.

Someone has to be home, she thought, knocking again.

After another few minutes, with still no answer, she grabbed the doorknob, twisting it until the door popped open. Her heart thumped. She didn't know if she was welcome or not; however, her need for answers far outweighed the risk of improper behavior.

"Hello?" she called out. Her voice echoed in the foyer. "Is anyone home? It's Miss Prescott. I'm here to see about the accident and how Roderick is. Hello?"

No one answered her back, and she spun around the foyer as if the movement would somehow find, even just a hint, that she wasn't alone as she presumed.

"I don't know who you think you are," a voice shouted from upstairs. She spun to find two men walking toward the railing.

"And I should say the same to you," the other man fired back at the first one.

"I'm the doctor in Lone Hollow. You are no one to me here."

"Well, I'm the doctor in Butte, and I should say I have more experience than someone who resides in a town such as this."

The first doctor, the one from Lone Hollow, shoved his hands on his hips. "So, you think just because you come from the city, you know more than I do? I've treated several burn patients in my life, and never have I done what you have done for Mr. Townsend. You must treat the burns. Not dope him up on laudanum and hope his body heals itself."

"I know what I'm doing!" the second doctor said.

"And so do I!"

The two men stood, toe-to-toe, staring at one another. Lily didn't know if she should interrupt, but the voice inside her, still begging for answers, screamed at her.

"Excuse me," she said.

The two men flinched and spun, gazing upon her.

"Who are you?" the second one asked.

She took a few steps backward toward the door, uneasy of the man's furious tone.

The first doctor moved around the second, heading toward her. "I think what Dr. Stevenson means is how may we help you?" He shot a glare over his shoulder at the second doctor, then turned back to Lily.

"I'm here to see Mr. Townsend, Zachary Townsend."

"I'm afraid Mr. Zachary Townsend doesn't live here anymore. He and Mrs. Townsend moved to Butte several weeks ago."

"What?" Lily clutched her throat. Had she traveled to Lone Hollow only to discover Roderick was in Butte? "Where is Roderick Townsend?"

"I'm afraid young Mr. Townsend is not up for company at this moment."

"So, he is alive?"

"Yes, he is."

Lily's knees grew weak. She thought to sit down for a moment but mustered up the strength to remain standing. It had been the news she'd longed to hear since she'd read the horrifying newspaper headline.

"I'm Dr. Fields, by the way." He stuck out his hand to shake Lily's. "I'm the doctor in Lone Hollow."

"Lily Prescott. I'm Roderick's . . . I'm his fiancée."

"Yes, I figured."

"How did you?"

"It's a small town, and word has a way of spreading through it." He offered her a wink.

"Where is he?" Lily asked; her tone had a hint of begging to it. "May I see him?"

"He's upstairs in his bedroom."

Lily moved around the man, but before she could pass him, he reached out and grabbed her arm. "Miss Prescott, if I may.

Please. I'm not sure you wish to see him. Not now and not in this condition."

"What condition?"

"I'm afraid Mr. Townsend was burned in the explosion."

"How bad are the burns?"

"They are along his arm and his torso. It could have been worse. But he is still in a lot of pain."

"Any infection? Have you tried Linseed oil and lime water?"

The doctor cocked his head to the side. "How . . ."

Lily ducked her chin. "Forgive the questions, Doctor. I have always had a fascination with medicine, and I have read journals my whole life. Well, the ones published I could get my hands on. I'm sure there are more I haven't seen."

"There is no apology necessary, Miss Prescott. I have done one treatment. I would do more, but . . ." Dr. Fields motioned to Dr. Stevenson, who rested his hands on his hips and had begun shaking his head.

"Needless treatment," Dr. Stevenson said. "There is no proof it works against the infection caused by burns."

"But there is proof. Dr. Montgomery published an article in the British Medical Journal, attesting to the research he did on his own brother and sister. The method has been used in England and Scotland."

"This is not England or Scotland!" Dr. Stevenson shouted, stepping toward Dr. Fields and Lily. "This is America. Now, I have been ordered to treat Mr. Townsend by his parents, and that is what I will do."

"And what about me?" Lily didn't know why she spoke, but something had spurred her to, and although her heart thumped, she clenched her fists as though doing so gave her courage. "Don't I have a say?"

"Are you his wife?"

"She is as good as," Dr. Fields said. "Which also means that this is her house . . . or it will be, and Mr. and Mrs. Townsend or not, since they no longer live here, she has the authority to ask you to leave."

"And what does she say then?" Dr. Stevenson puffed his chest as though he wanted to appear bigger than he was. His voice deepened in a tone that screamed intimidation. Lily hated the tone. It was as though he was trying to make her sound inferior.

Dr. Fields looked at her. "Miss Prescott? How would you like to proceed?"

Lily paused, remembering the article she'd read about burn treatments as well as remembering how the girl had stopped screaming when she and Miss Whittaker helped her after the water burn. She didn't want to make a mistake with either doctor, but her gut feeling raised the loudest ruckus in her chest, and she opened her mouth, blurting out the words before she even had a moment to think about them first.

"Thank you for your help, Dr. Stevenson. However, I'm going to have to ask you to leave. Dr. Fields is more than capable, and I am employing his help to treat my fiancé from now on."

Dr. Stevenson folded his arms across his chest. "That's fine. I'm sure I will be back as soon as Mr. and Mrs. Townsend hear of this."

Before either Lily or Dr. Fields could say another word, he spun and left the room, headed toward the kitchen, where, after a few moments, the door slammed, and he left.

Lily inhaled and exhaled several deep breaths. She didn't know if she'd make a mistake or not, but she couldn't think about it. Not now.

"May I see him?"

"Yes. And while you're with him, I shall prepare some more wool strips for another treatment. I must warn you; he's had laudanum, so he's a little out of it."

"I understand."

***

Lily followed Dr. Fields up the stairs. It felt like she'd just been at the house, even though weeks had passed.

"May I ask you something?" she asked the doctor.

"Of course."

"You mentioned Mr. and Mrs. Townsend no longer live here, and this was essentially my house. What did you mean?"

"Mr. and Mrs. Townsend moved to Butte several weeks ago, and young Mr. Townsend is the only one here now after his father gave him the house, the business. It was the talk of the town for days. Well, that and you leaving. No one knew where you went."

Lily ducked her chin and lowered her voice. "I was in Butte."

"Well, it is good you are here now."

"Do you know what happened?"

"The boiler exploded." The doctor paused, scratching his forehead with his fingers. "Mr. Linwood died, and two other men who rushed in to get Mr. Linwood out of the way."

Lily's heart sank. She'd spent only an afternoon with the older gentleman, but even in those few hours, she became fond of Mr. Linwood. He was such a kind man, and she knew how much he loved his wife.

They reached Roderick's bedroom door, and the doctor hesitated for a moment before opening it. Lily followed him inside, stopping as she saw Roderick lying on the bed. A blanket covered his legs while the top half of his body was uncovered. His skin looked raw and red, and it oozed.

"He looks like he's in pain."

"He is. Well, somewhat. The laudanum is helping. I shall go downstairs and ready the treatment. Will you help with applying it when I bring it up?"

"Of course."

While Dr. Fields left the room and headed back downstairs, Lily made her way to Roderick's bedside and kneeled.

"Roderick?" she whispered.

He turned his head toward her, and a faint smile spread across his face. He opened his mouth to talk, but she shook her head and pressed her finger to her lips.

"No, say nothing. I don't want you to be in any more pain. I just wanted you to know I'm here, and I'm going to help Dr. Fields in any way I can."

He smiled again and nodded slightly. His head moved only a little before he closed his eyes.

Lily stayed by the bed until Dr. Fields returned with a tray, and as he set it down, the two began to work, soaking the strips of wool in the oils and laying them on Roderick. He winced with every one but then seemed to calm down after they were finished.

"Now, what do we do?" she asked the doctor.

"Now? We wait."

FIFTEEN

LILY

The teacups rattled on the tray as Lily carried it up the stairs and into Roderick's bedroom.

"Good morning," she said to him as she entered.

"Good morning." He sat up, pulling the blanket up over his chest as he leaned against the pillows and headboard. A broad grin spread across his face as she made her way over to the bed and set the tray on the bedside table, pushing the books he'd laid there last night out of the way. "You know, you don't have to keep spoiling me. I can get out of bed and get my own tea."

"Ah." She held up a finger, wiggling it. "You may be able to do it, but that doesn't mean you should."

"But I've been lying in this bed for months, and Dr. Fields said that getting up and around is good for me. At least a little each day."

"Nevertheless, I know when you push yourself, and yesterday you did too much."

"What if I agreed not to overdo it? Would you release those reins you have held tight in your hands?"

Her eyes narrowed, and she cocked her head to the side,

looking down on him with just moving her eyes and not her head. "I suppose that is something I can agree to."

"Good."

She turned her attention to the tea, pouring him a cup and adding sugar and cream, stirring the liquid into a pale brown color before handing it to him.

"You know, before you came along, I didn't care for cream or sugar."

"Really?"

"No. I just drank it without. I guess I didn't know what I was missing."

"I can't drink it without. Just like coffee."

"I can still drink black coffee." He chuckled slightly under his breath, and after she handed him the cup, he took a sip as he placed the saucer in his lap, then set the cup down. "How was the funeral?" he asked.

"Sad." She took her seat in the chair she'd parked near the bed the first night she arrived back in Lone Hollow and settled down into the soft cushions. "I felt so awful for Mrs. Linwood."

"I can't imagine how she feels." Roderick stared at his cup, ducking his chin as he lowered his voice. Sadness oozed through his words. "I'm going to miss Mr. Linwood more than I thought I would."

"He was a good man."

"He was the best." Roderick glanced at her. "Did you know he'd been working for the sawmill for twelve years?"

"Really? That long?"

"Yeah. He started when I was a boy and worked his way up to the head sawyer." Roderick paused, hesitating for a moment. "Did my parents . . . were they at the funeral?"

Although she didn't want to answer his question, she knew she had to, and she shook her head.

"So, I wasn't there, and they weren't there. No one from the . . . I should have been there."

"Mrs. Linwood wasn't angry that you weren't. She even told me she understood. She just wants you to get better. She didn't mind that you weren't there."

"It matters to me." Roderick raised his voice but then lowered it. "I want to visit her. As soon as she will have company."

"All right. I will write to her this afternoon. Or if I see her in town, I will ask her to let us know when she will be up for a visit."

"And did you give her the envelope I asked you to give her?"

"Yes. She was relieved. Without her husband's income . . . I think she was a bit lost with not knowing what she was going to do."

"Well, I'm still going to cover his wages. I don't care what my father says. That woman and her children will not be left in the poorhouse because of the accident."

"And she appreciates that, and I will help you make sure that she gets it."

Roderick seemed to tense up for a moment, then he softened and leaned his head back onto his pillow. He exhaled a deep breath, then looked at Lily once more. A smile reappeared on his face. "I am happy you came back."

"Me too, and I'm sorry—"

"No. There will be no apologies. Not from you. I'm sorry that my mother and Emily did that to you that night."

"And I'm sorry I didn't believe you." She held up her hand to stop him from speaking. "No, I do need to say sorry for that. You tried to tell me, and I didn't believe you."

"I can see why you would have reason not to."

"Really? Because I don't. You showed me nothing but kindness and love." She paused a moment, softening her voice. "I want you to know I'll never not believe you again."

"So, does this mean you will stay in Lone Hollow?"

"Only if you will have me."

He cocked his head to the side. "Do you think Pastor Duncan will marry us right here in this bedroom?"

She laughed. "I think if we asked him to, he would be more than happy to oblige us."

"You still have your ring, right?"

She held up her hand. Although she hadn't worn it after returning to the orphanage, she had slipped it on when she left to return to Lone Hollow, and there, on her finger, it had remained.

He nodded. "And there it will stay, right?"

"Always."

He smiled for the third time, and his eyes narrowed playfully. "I want to take you somewhere," he said.

"Where is that?"

"It's a surprise. Will you go with me?"

"Of course."

~

The wagon wheels rolled down the lane until they reached a small house in the trees. The place wasn't new, but it wasn't rundown either. It had a sense of depth to it. Like something from a dream. A warm place that one could call home. She just didn't know who that one was. Was this going to be their house?

Lily glanced at the forest around them, and she lifted her hand to shield the sun from her eyes. "Where are we?" she asked.

"Before I answer that, can I have your word that you will keep an open mind?"

His question twisted in her stomach. "What do you mean?"

"I would never ask you to do something you didn't wish to do. However, in this case . . . in this case, I'm afraid I need to break that vow."

"Roderick, where are we? Is this our house?"

"No. This is the home of Mr. Allen Prescott."

A lump formed in her throat, and although she tried to swallow it, she couldn't. It was lodged too far and too deep, and the fact that her eyes were misted with tears didn't help.

"Is . . . is he expecting us?"

"No, he's not. So, if you wish for me to turn around, I will. However, I don't think we should. I think you need this, and I think he needs this."

"What if he doesn't wish to know me?"

"Then we will deal with that when the time comes. I do know a little about the man, though, and I don't think he would turn you away."

She sucked in a breath, nodding at Roderick. "All right. All right, I will do it. I will tell him."

She continued to nod, more as a distraction than anything, as Roderick cued the horse to continue up to the house. Her heart thumped, and while she tried to think of what she was going to say, words failed her and created nothing but a mess in her mind.

As the wagon halted in front of the house, the door opened, and Mr. Prescott stepped outside. "Good afternoon, Mr. Townsend. How are you today?"

"I'm doing well, Mr. Prescott. How are you?"

"Oh, just fine. Same as always. Anything I can do for you?"

"Well, actually, I came here to do something for you." Roderick climbed out of the wagon, motioning for Lily to follow him, then helping her down. Her legs trembled as she steadied her feet on the ground, and, for a moment, she feared her knees would give out. She grabbed Roderick to help her balance, and he reached for her hand, clutching it into his as he led her over to Mr. Prescott.

"Something you can do for me, huh? And what's that?"

"Well, first . . . have you met my fiancée? Mr. Prescott, this is

Miss Lily . . . Miss Lily Prescott."

"Oh, how do you—" The man's eyes widened, and he sucked in a breath. "Your last name is Prescott?"

Lily nodded. "It wasn't my mother's, though. She gave me my father's name when I was born, but they weren't married."

"And what was your mother's name?"

"Cecilia . . . Cecilia Crestwood. And I believe I'm your daughter."

Mr. Prescott stumbled back until his backside hit the wall of his house. His mouth gaped open, and he clutched his chest as though he were trying to clutch his heart.

"You . . . it's you. It's you." His words were like whispers on his lips and his eyes filled with tears that streamed down his cheeks.

"Yes, it's me," she said.

He dropped to his knees, burying his face in his hands. "I didn't think I would ever meet you."

She darted for him, kneeling in front of him. "You knew about me?"

"I knew your mother was pregnant. We were just foolish children back then, but we loved each other. We made a choice one night, and after, although it was what we both wanted, we vowed never to do it again, at least until we were married, but it was too late. You came from that choice. We were both so happy. But her parents were not. They took her away from me, and I never heard from her again. I didn't know if you were a boy or a girl, if she kept you or if they sent you to live with another family. I knew of you. But I knew nothing about you."

"So, you . . . you wanted me?"

"Wanted you? Of course, I wanted you. I wanted you and your mother. I wanted to marry her and raise you and for us to be a family. But my choice . . . it was taken from me. They took it from me." He glanced up at her. Tears still streamed down his face, and his eyes were red and had already puffed up.

"I'm so sorry they did that."

"Your mother? How is she? Where is she?"

Lily's heart sank. She didn't know how to tell this man her mother was dead. "I'm . . . I'm sorry to have to tell you, but she died."

"When?"

"About thirteen years ago."

"What happened?"

"I don't know. She got sick, and she couldn't care for me. She left me at an orphanage in Butte."

"You've been in Butte all this time? Why didn't she write to me? I stayed here in Lone Hollow because I thought she would come back. Did she tell you much about me?"

"Unfortunately, no. She didn't tell me hardly anything at all. I don't know why. It was only until she left me at the orphanage that she gave me a slip of paper with your name and where you lived."

He looked at her again, then wiped his eyes and face. "Then God did the rest when he brought you here and to Mr. Townsend."

"Yes, He did."

"Does this mean you are staying in Lone Hollow?"

"Yes, I am."

He sucked in a breath and reached out, clutching her hand in his. "Then I very much would like to get to know you. If that is all right with you."

"It's more than all right."

Although a part of her wasn't sure and asked her to hesitate, the other part of her screamed not to care. She listened to the latter and leaned toward him, wrapping her arms around him in a tight embrace. He returned her hug, and although he sobbed at first, his sobs soon turned into laughter—laughter that made her laugh too.

She finally found her father.

SIXTEEN

LILY

*L*ily adjusted the pin in her hair and looked at her reflection in the mirror. She and Roderick had waited several long months before having the wedding in order for him to heal, and as the day finally neared, the more she found herself excited, and yet, wishing it was already over. Not because she dreaded the day or didn't wish to enjoy it. But because she was ready to start their lives together.

No more staying in the guest house.

No more planning.

No more waiting.

She was ready to wake up as Mrs. Roderick Townsend and happily live for the rest of her life with that very title.

With the flowers secured among her pinned tresses, she stood from the vanity and brushed the lace of her dress straight. It had been a gift, sent to her by Mrs. Meyer along with a note, not only apologizing for such a rude dismissal but also letting Lily know that had Mrs. Meyer known the details of what Miss Sanderson had done; she wouldn't have dismissed Lily from the dress shop quite as easily.

Not that Lily cared much any more.

What did it matter?

Emily Sanderson, she had heard, was now Mrs. Stewart Dowery, and although the marriage had happened only a few short months ago, there were rumors—brought to Lily's ears via Mrs. Townsend, of trouble brewing in the young couple. Lily had paid little attention to the reasons; however, she could guess perhaps Stewart finally learned precisely the type of woman he married.

Of course, Lily never cared much for gossip, let alone gossip brought to her attention by Mrs. Townsend. Still, she sat in the company of Roderick's parents anyway, listening to his mother go on and on as a way of at least trying to bury the hatchet. It certainly wouldn't be a kindred friendship, but it would be one as daughter-in-law and mother-in-law—at least in some manner of speaking.

A knock rapped on her bedroom door, and as she turned to tell whoever it was to come in, the door popped open a crack.

"Lily? Are you ready?" her father asked.

"Yes. You can come in."

He opened the door a bit more, stepping inside and stopping in his tracks as he laid his gaze upon her. He heaved a deep sigh. "You . . . you are stunning."

"Thank you."

"I've come to see if you are ready as they are waiting for you downstairs."

"All right. I am ready." She moved toward him. "It isn't too cold outside, is it?"

"Nope." Allen shook his head, then ran his hand through his hair. "It's a perfect fall day. It seems God wished to bless you with pleasant weather . . . even in October."

She smiled. "Well, I guess then it's time to get married."

She looped her arm through his, and he led her out of the guest house and toward the clearing in the trees where she and Roderick picked to get married.

Nearly half the town was already there and standing while they waited for her.

As they reached the aisle, Allen stopped and glanced at her, pausing for a moment before walking her down to meet her forever. "Seems odd to finally get you back, only to give you away again," he said.

She glanced at him, then at Roderick, who was waiting at the end with a grin etched across his face. "You aren't giving me away, though. At least not in the sense that you are losing a daughter. You're just gaining a son."

"Then I guess God has blessed me twice today." With the last of his words, Allen's grip on her arm tightened, and he walked her down the aisle, handing her arm over to Roderick after shaking his hand. The young man slightly trembled and heaved a sigh as Lily took her stance beside him.

"You look beautiful," he whispered.

"And you look handsome."

"Are you ready to get married?"

"Darling, I've been ready since the moment you proposed."

"I suppose my father didn't make a mistake after all, did he?"

"If it was . . . it was the best one anyone has ever made."

THE END

LOVE HER MAIL ORDER MISTAKE?

READ BOOK THREE OF THE BRIDES OF LONE HOLLOW

A woman who thinks she's the new teacher . . .

A male teacher who placed an advertisement for a bride and not his replacement . . .

And a bet of all bets—win over the town and become the teacher of Lone Hollow.

Order or read for FREE with Kindle Unlimited

Her Mail Order Misunderstanding

Turn the page for a sneak peek at Book Three in the Brides of Lone Hollow Series

ONE

HARRISON

Those who have never met anyone stubborn obviously haven't met Colt Reiner.

It was a thought Harrison Craig thought to himself more than once on a daily basis, and looking at the six-year-old, standing with his arms folded near a tree while his mama knelt in front of him, a thought he was sure his parents thought as well.

How could anyone not? Coming in contact with that child was like standing on the train tracks, holding their hand up, all the while thinking that they would have the power to stop a train chugging down the tracks at full speed.

Honestly, Harrison thought the person trying to stop the train had better odds at times.

And from the look on Colt's mama's face, she might agree.

Watching the poor woman, Harrison had to chuckle to himself before he turned his attention back to the table of homemade pies, cakes, and an arrangement of cookies so loaded with sugar they made his teeth hurt just thinking about tasting them.

"Mr. Craig! Mr. Craig! Have you tried my pie?" Sadie

McCray came bounding toward her teacher. Her white-blonde curls bounced, and a smile spread across her face.

"I haven't yet, Sadie," Harrison answered. He paused for a moment, but then, taking in the sight of how fast her smile faded and disappointment flooded her face, he continued. "But I'd love to try some now. Do you think you could fetch me a slice?"

Her smile returned. "Of course, Mr. Craig. I'll be right back."

She darted off to one of the other tables filled with desserts. While it had been a wonderful idea to host a picnic for the children and parents at the start of the new school year, he hadn't thought to make sure families brought an array of dishes for everyone to eat. With little word on what to bring, everyone brought dessert, leaving an endless number of tables full of sugar and only a few platters of meats, cheeses, and bread. Trays that emptied within minutes.

Until then, it had been a secret that while Harrison was a master at teaching the children, his party planning skills lacked . . .severely.

"Good afternoon, Mr. Craig," a voice said behind him.

He turned to see Maggie and Cullen McCray approaching them, and he nodded, shaking Mr. McCray's hand.

"Good afternoon to you both."

"I saw Sadie dart off in another direction. Did she say hello to you?" Mr. McCray asked.

"Yes, she did. She is getting me a piece of her pie."

"Ah, I see. Well, I have to say that you are in for a treat, and I'm not even being biased. She's turned into quite the little baker in the last few months."

"Then I shall look forward to the slice coming."

"We wanted to ask you how she is doing with her schooling," Mrs. McCray said. She cocked her head slightly as her husband wrapped his arm around her waist. Harrison followed the movement, trying not to watch, but failing.

While it had been a secret, he wasn't much of a planner when it came to town functions; it was also a town secret about how much he longed for a wife of his own.

"She's doing excellent now that she's caught up."

"That's wonderful to hear. She talks non-stop about you and how much you have helped her."

"Well, she's a good girl, and she's learned quickly. I've had other children who weren't as far behind on their studies take months longer to catch up. You both should be proud."

"I am proud," Mr. McCray said, heaving a deep sigh. "Though I also am feeling guilty about letting her schooling slip as I did. Thankfully, this woman," he squeezed Mrs. McCray a little tighter, and the woman smiled, ducking her chin. "Put me in my place when it came to what the girl needed."

"I'm sure you would have figured it out if she hadn't. But there's always something to the orders of a woman that does wonders for us stubborn men." Harrison glanced over at Colt's mama, who was still kneeling in front of her son. A slight laugh snorted through his nose. "At least some of us men."

"Here you go, Mr. Craig," Sadie said, trotting back over to the three of them. The slice of pie bounced a little on the plate and tipped over as she halted in front of her teacher. Her cheeks turned pink, and she gave him a sheepish grin. "Sorry."

"It's quite all right. I'm sure it won't affect the taste at all. Besides, it all gets jumbled up in the mouth and stomach anyway, right?"

"Right."

He took the plate and fork from her, digging into his first bite while she watched. Her eyes were the size of the plate, and she bit her lip as though she waited on bated breath to see how much he liked it.

The sugar, cinnamon, and apples hit his tongue with a sweet but tart jolt, and it blended perfectly with the flaky, buttery crust that all seemed to melt in his mouth.

"This is by far the best pie I've ever tasted, Sadie," he said.

A beaming smile spread across her face, and she grabbed the sides of her dress, holding them out to give him a curtsy. "Thank you."

She turned toward Mr. and Mrs. McCray. "I told you he would like it."

"And we never doubted you," Mr. McCray said. "Now, find your friends and play. We will leave in about an hour to head home."

"But do we have to?" She stuck out her bottom lip in a pout.

"Yes, now, run along before I change my mind, and we leave now."

Before Mr. McCray finished his sentence, she spun on her heel and darted off toward the play yard near the school where all the other children were playing. Her hair whipped from her haste, and she vanished before Harrison had a chance even to take another bite of pie.

"I have to say," he said to the McCray's. "This is the best pie I've ever eaten. She has amazing skills."

"Yes, she does. She's taken over most of the cooking in the house. Which I have to say has been a blessing at times when I haven't felt good." Mrs. McCray rubbed her hand over the small, growing bump of her stomach.

It was another move Harrison couldn't help but watch with a longing in his chest. He loved children—which was a given with his profession. Why would someone go into teaching if they didn't? But it was more than just loving how he helped shape the minds of the children he taught. He wanted children of his own. Boys, girls, it didn't matter. One, two, ten, the number didn't matter either. He just wanted a wife and a family. Period.

"Well, we won't keep any more of your time. We just wanted to extend our appreciation and see how she's doing."

The pair wandered off, leaving Harrison standing next to the table with a lonely little piece of half-eaten pie. There was nothing but families surrounding him. Mothers and fathers, husbands and wives, and although he often found himself as the odd man out, single and alone, there were only a few times the feeling had ever hit him this hard in the chest.

And today was one of those times.

"Mr. McCray?" He called after the pair, darting after them too as they both turned to face him. He glanced at Mrs. McCray, and his cheeks flushed with warmth. He couldn't ask with her listening. "Uh, might I have a word with you . . . alone?"

The two of them looked at each other, and Mrs. McCray smiled, releasing her husband's arm. "Why don't I fetch myself a slice of that pie? Perhaps I can keep it down this time without retching it back up in an hour."

As she walked off, the two men watched her. Harrison's heart raced. He didn't know how Mr. McCray would take the question, and he also didn't want to look like a fool.

"What is it you wish to speak to me about, Mr. Craig?"

"Well, I was wondering . . . if you don't mind my asking . . . where did you and Mrs. McCray meet?"

Mr. McCray blinked a few times, then he inhaled and exhaled a deep breath. "Well, it's funny you should ask. She came to Lone Hollow to marry Clint, my brother. She left her home before word could reach her about his death. I don't know how I could be blessed with such a miracle, but I thank God every day he gave me another chance."

"So, you didn't correspond with her before?"

"No. And I never asked her how she met Clint. I could if you wished for me to ask."

The warmth spread down Harrison's neck, and he shook his head. "Oh, no. No, that won't be necessary. I was just curious."

Mr. McCray studied him for a moment and the man's eyes narrowed. "You know, if you are looking for information on . . . women to correspond with, you might wish to speak to Mr.

Townsend. It was rumored that his father sent for Lily through a marriage broker or something like that. I'm sure he could get you in touch with whoever it was his father had contact with."

"Oh. All right. I suppose I will talk to him. Thank you."

Mr. McCray offered a smile and clapped his hand on Harrison's back. "Glad to have helped. Even if it was only a little." He moved forward a few steps, then turned to face Harrison again. "For the record, Mr. Craig. Having a wife and family . . . is more than I could have ever hoped for, and it's nothing to be embarrassed about if such is what you desire for yourself."

Harrison ducked his chin, giving a nod. "Thank you."

"Oh, and if you're looking for Mr. Townsend. He is over with Mayor Jackson. They are talking about plans to do . . . something. I'm not sure what. All I know is when those two get together; it usually ends up costing everyone in town money." Mr. McCray snorted a laugh, and with a slight wave, he strode off toward Mrs. McCray, who stood at the table, shoveling bites of pie into her mouth as though she hadn't seen food in days.

***

Just as Mr. McCray had said, Harrison found Mr. Townsend and Mayor Jackson over near the school. Lost in their conversation, both of their arms waved in the air excitedly, and as he caught their attention, they waved him over.

"Ah, Mr. Craig, we were just going to come find you. We wanted to know what your opinion is about expanding the school," Mayor Jackson said.

"Expanding? But we haven't outgrown it. In fact, there is room for plenty more children before that happens."

"Well, yes, I am aware of that matter. However, Lone Hollow is growing, and I thought we should grab the bull by the horns, so to speak, and be proactive on expanding the school when the town has a surplus of money to fund it, instead of after something happens and there is no budget to spend."

"But then what will happen if there is an emergency?"

"Oh, that's not something we should concern ourselves with. My focus is expanding the school so that Lone Hollow can continue to grow. More and more people are moving here, ya know. We might even need a second teacher one of these days."

"A second teacher?"

Mayor Jackson shrugged. "You never know." The plump man pointed his fat finger in Harrison's face and wiggled it. "And you would benefit from the help, too. Not that I think you're overworked. But having another teacher around can't be that bad."

"Yes, I know."

"Then it's settled."

"What is? Are you going to write for another teaching post?"

"Heavens, no. At least not yet anyway. No, I meant the plans to expand the schoolhouse. I shall start the plans first thing in the morning." He turned to Mr. Townsend, who had been over-hearing the conversation, but who also had looked a little distracted with studying the dimensions of the schoolhouse. "And, Mr. Townsend, I will be in touch as soon as I know the amount of lumber we will need."

"I'll be waiting for the command to start, then."

"Yes, please do. Now, if you both will excuse me. I heard a charming little girl going on about her apple pie earlier, and I must say, listening to her made my mouth water. I'm going to see if I can find myself a piece. If there is any left, I mean."

Harrison watched as Mayor Jackson meandered over to the tables, scouring them all until he found the pie tin he'd obviously been looking for. A broad grin spread across the man's face, and he scooped up a slice, dumping it on a plate before grabbing a fork and digging in.

"Sometimes I don't know about that man's choices as Mayor," Mr. Townsend said, watching him, too.

Harrison snorted a laugh. "You and everyone else in this town. But somehow, we all voted for him, anyway."

"That's the odd part, is it not?" Mr. Townsend glanced at Harrison, and the two laughed.

"Do you think it will be expensive to expand the school?" Harrison asked.

Mr. Townsend shook his head. "No. I'll make sure that it's not. It will be my contribution to the school, considering you might be teaching my son or daughter when the time comes."

"So, Lily is . . ."

"Yes. We believe so."

"Congratulations."

"Thank you. We've been trying since the wedding last Fall, and while we didn't think it would happen so quickly, we are quite happy."

Harrison glanced over at the young man standing next to him, and while it wasn't a sense of jealously that plagued him, there was something there. Something he felt in his chest that almost made it hurt. Perhaps it was longing.

"Mr. Townsend, may I ask you something?" he asked.

"Of course."

"I was speaking to Mr. McCray, and he mentioned how you met Lily. Is it true?"

"That my father sent for her, and she was a mail-order bride?"

"Well, he didn't say those words exactly, but yes."

Mr. Townsend nodded and gave a slight smirk. "I'm not sure if I should be impressed with the gossip or embarrassed." He paused, chuckling again before he continued. "But to answer your question, yes, it is true. My father went through a marriage broker named Mr. Benson. I can get you the information if you would like."

"Oh, I don't know if I want to go through Mr. Benson just yet. I was just curious."

Mr. Townsend slapped Harrison on the back. "I'll tell you what, why don't I write to Mr. Benson asking him if he has a young lady looking to correspond with a nice gentleman. If he does and writes back, then you can decide if you want to contact her. Sound all right?"

Harrison bit his lip for a moment. While the embarrassed part of him wanted to say no, the other part of him that longed for a wife and family screamed to say yes.

The latter won.

"All right. Thank you."

"It's not a problem. Now all I have to do is figure out how we are going to expand this schoolhouse."

TWO

AMELIA

*A*melia stumbled up to the schoolhouse door, dropping the books she had stacked in her arms. They hit the ground with a thud, and she groaned as she glanced up at the sky. "A little help, here," she said. "Just a little help."

The early morning air chilled through her jacket, and the dew from the fog that rolled in overnight dampened not only her dress but the strands of her hair. She brushed her dark chocolate curls out of her face, ignoring how some hairs stuck to her cheeks as she bent down and fetched the books. The ones that landed on the bottom were covered in dirt.

"Just a little help," she said again—her tone more like a whisper on her annoyed breath.

After picking the books up and dusting off the dirty ones, she tucked them back under her arms and turned the doorknob, entering the schoolhouse and heading toward her desk without bothering to close the door.

It was the start of another school year, and the start to what she hoped would be a better year.

With the books laid down on her desk, she moved around to the other side of the room, heading to the stove to not only light it but to add a bit of wood and kindling to reignite the fire. Her hot breath was visible in the cold room, and her fingers fumbled with the match, trembling as she lit it and then stuck it in the stove, watching as the flame burned the pine needles into nothing but black strings of charred bits and ignited the pinecones and chunks of wood.

She wanted to stand by the stove for the rest of the morning, but she knew she couldn't, and she moved over toward the blackboard, ignoring how the hairs on her arms stood in search of the warmth as she walked away from the stove. She grabbed a piece of chalk, writing a few sentences that she would have to teach that day.

Someone cleared their throat behind her, and she jumped, spinning to face the sound. She clutched her chest, letting out a sigh.

"Mayor Sheffield. You scared me."

"I'm sorry, Miss Hawthorn. I didn't mean to. I should have announced myself at the door." The older gentleman ducked his chin and removed the hat from his head.

"It's not a bother. What can I do for you, Mr. Sheffield?"

His brow furrowed, and he opened his mouth, only to close it before he said a word.

Her stomach twisted. "Don't tell me no students are coming to school today."

"I'm afraid there aren't. All but Billy and Suzy have moved away and now . . . well, Samuel's folks think he'd be better off doing his schooling at home so he can tend to more chores."

"More chores? Because this country functions on chores."

"Well, it kind of does. At least out here, it does."

"And so all children are just supposed to stay here in Brook Creek. A town that is losing residents daily. Pretty soon, there won't be anyone living here at all."

"You think I don't know that? What can we do, though? The water is drying up and with other towns like Lone Hollow growing as they are . . . I can't keep people from wanting to live someplace where they can have a better life. Not to mention some of the newcomers who have moved here. Only men without wives or children, and some don't look right. Like something's wrong with them."

Although Amelia wanted to disagree with the mayor, she knew she couldn't. She knew how the town was suffering to survive. So many families had already moved away, and the ones who remained . . . it was only a matter of time before they would be gone, too. She also knew of the men the mayor spoke of, and they had worried her too from time to time. Seedy types, only here to look for a drink in the saloon or a girl to warm their beds. It was getting so she didn't even wish to be out at night alone.

"So, that's it. What am I supposed to do?"

The mayor ducked his chin again, letting out another deep sigh as his shoulders hunched and he paced the floor of the schoolhouse. "I'm sorry to have to tell you this, Miss Hawthorn, but with no children . . . I have to close the schoolhouse."

Amelia sucked in a breath. She had a feeling this day was coming. The problem was, however, she had no other post—and no other job—to take.

What would she do now?

She couldn't return to the city. Not only had she no place to live, but she had no money to return home. She'd spent every last dime she had traveling to Brook Creek and hadn't had much pay since. It took all she had just to rent a small room from one of the families and keep food on her table.

"So, what is it you're saying, Mr. Sheffield? Are you saying I'm now out of a job?"

The older man paused and inhaled a breath. His belly stuck out several inches farther for a moment before he exhaled. "Well, I'm afraid so."

Tears misted her eyes, and she turned away from him,

nodding. It was the only thing she could think to do through her shock. Fighting back the tears, she gathered the schoolbooks from the desks and stacked them on the bookshelf in the corner. A few of them had pencil marks on them from the few different children she had taught in the few months she'd lived in Brook Creek. While she never wanted to get too attached to them—it was always too hard if and when the time came, she would have to say goodbye—she couldn't deny, her heart broke a little with the sight of all the letters of their names.

"Because I knew this day was coming," Mayor Sheffield said. "I wrote to Mrs. Seymore about another post for you. She . . . she sent this, and it arrived this afternoon."

As Amelia turned and faced him, he stepped toward her, outstretching his hand to hand over an envelope.

"What is it?"

"I'm not sure."

She flipped it over in her hand and opened it, sliding the folded piece of parchment from the depths. She unfolded it, reading the letter from Mrs. Seymore.

My dearest Amelia,

What a mess I've made in sending you to such a small town. Please forgive me. Mayor Sheffield has made me aware of the situation, and after some digging, I have found some news that I think you might be happy to hear.

When you were hired as a teacher, you inquired about a post in the town of Lone Hollow. While I don't have all the details yet, I have heard rumors of an advertisement coming in from the local teacher of the town. There has been no formal request that I know of; however, I will make sure to let anyone know when it comes in, I have filled the post. If I were you, I would relocate to Lone Hollow as soon as you receive this and wait for my instructions to come.

I sincerely hope this letter finds you well outside of this predicament, and I look forward to writing to you with all the details as soon as they are given to me.

Sincerely,
Mrs. Jane Seymore

Amelia read the letter a second time and then a third. While she was still heartbroken over the town she'd just spent the last year in, she also couldn't help but feel a swell of excitement. She'd hoped and prayed for the post in Lone Hollow for a long time, and now it was hers.

It was finally hers.

"I am to leave for Lone Hollow," she said to Mayor Sheffield.

The older man smiled and nodded. "At least some good news came from this."

"Yes, it did. I am still sad for Brook Creek, though. Sad for the town, for the people. I loved the children I taught while I was here, and I hope I made them enjoy school."

"I'm sure you did." He gave her another nod, then motioned toward her desk. "I'll let you pack up. Take your time. I'll lock up the schoolhouse later this afternoon."

He watched her for a bit, then left the schoolhouse, leaving the scent of his aftershave as the only remnant that he'd been in the room with her.

Finally alone, she gathered the crate she'd kept in the corner and began packing away her books. Each one rested on the one below it until they all were stacked inside. With those packed, she took to the rest of her belongings and stuffed them away in her bag before extinguishing the stove, grabbing the crate, and heading to the door of the school, shutting it behind her for the last time.

The little white building—once a place of hope and a sense of future—now felt hollow. Even if she had a new post to look forward to, there was a sense of loss and sadness, like a disappointment that leaves a wound and never heals right.

I suppose that will be what Brook Creek will be, she thought to herself. A wound that will never heal right.

Her only hope now lay in another town and a teaching post she'd wanted for so long. It was finally hers, and in her excitement, as she walked away from her old schoolhouse, she couldn't even bring herself to glance over her shoulder. She didn't want to look at the past. Not anymore. No, all she wanted to do was look to the future.

The future in Lone Hollow.

ORDER OR READ FOR FREE WITH KINDLE UNLIMITED
HER MAIL ORDER MISUNDERSTANDING

WAGON TRAIN WOMEN

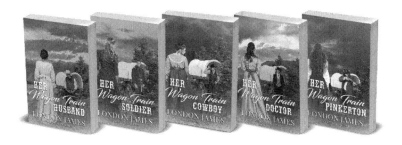

Five women headed out West to make new lives on the Frontier find hope and love in the arms of five men. Their adventures may be different, but their bond is the same as they embark on the journey together in the same wagon train.

CHECK OUT THE SERIES ON AMAZON!

Turn the page for a sneak peek at book one, Her Wagon Train Husband.

ONE

ABBY

*W*ell, almost everyone.

Abby had to correct herself on that point. Her parents didn't like adventure much. Neither did her three older sisters. They liked being home. They liked being in a place they knew. They didn't enjoy the thrill of the unknown or the sense that the world could open up right under their feet.

Of course, that wasn't an appealing thought. For surely that would mean death. And Abby didn't like the idea of that. She just liked the adventure.

Yeah, she thought to herself. I don't like that.

Abby heaved a deep sigh as she walked along the path around the lake. It was a favorite pastime for her and one she enjoyed nearly every day. Well, every day that her parents and sister's stayed in their country home. When they were in the city . . . well, that was another story. She would often sneak out of the house and head to the park. Even if she had to be careful about being seen, she would still try to get in a little walk in the trees and sunshine. Wasn't that what Spring and Summer were for? Perhaps even Autumn? Winter surely not, although she couldn't complain too much about those months. For she loved the snow too and would enjoy it until her fingers and nose turned red, and her skin hurt.

Something about nature called to her like a mother calls to a child when they want them to come home or to the table to sit down and share a meal. She loved everything about it. The smell of the air, the sound of the birds, and the leaves rustling in the breeze. The feel of the sunshine upon her skin and how it felt as though her body tried to soak it all in like a rag soaks up water.

The outdoors made her feel alive.

Much like the sense of adventure did.

And the two, she thought, went hand in hand.

"Aammeelliiaa!" She heard a woman's voice call out in the distance. Her name was long and drawn out and sounded as though the woman—her mother—calling had her hands up against the sides of her mouth.

Her heart thumped. She couldn't be caught coming from the direction of the lake, and yet, there would be no chance to sneak around to the other side of the stables without being seen. Her mother called for her several more times, and as she tried to round the stables, appearing as though she came from a different direction, she heard her mother's foot stomp on the front port.

"Abby Lynn Jacobson! And just where have you been?" Her mother raised her hand as if to stop her from answering. "Don't even tell me you were walking around that lake all by yourself."

"All right." Abby squared her shoulders. "I don't tell you that."

Her mother's eyes narrowed, and she pointed her finger in Abby's face. "You listen to me, young lady; you will not go flittering off again. Do you understand me? You have far too many responsibilities in this house to do anything other than what you're supposed to be doing."

"But sewing and cooking and cleaning are just so boring. I want to be outside."

"Outside is no place for a woman unless they are out there to hang laundry on the line or gardening. Both of which you need to be doing too." Her mother continued to wave her hands around the outside of the house, pointing toward the laundry line and the fenced garden around the back of the house. Clothes already hung on the line, and they moved in the breeze. "Your sisters certainly don't spend any time fooling around outside."

"That's because my sisters are married and have husbands to look after."

"And you will have one too. Sooner than later, now that your father has made it official."

"What do you mean?" Abby jerked her head, and her brow furrowed.

"Mr. Herbert Miller is on his way over to the house this afternoon."

"Why?" Although she asked, she wasn't sure she wanted the answer, nor did she believe she would like it.

Her mother shook her head and rolled her eyes. "To finalize the agreement and plans to marry you and take care of you, of course."

Abby sucked in a breath and spit went down the wrong pipe. She choked and sputtered, coughing several times while she gasped. "I . . . I . . ." She coughed a few more times and held out her hand until she regained composure. "I don't want to marry him."

"That's not for you to decide. He comes from a well-to-do family and intends to provide a good life for you. Not to mention we could use the money." Her mother clasped her hands together and fidgeted with her fingers as she glanced around the home. It was still in good shape for its age, but even Abby had seen some of the repairs it needed, and she knew her parents couldn't afford it. "I dare say he's the richest young man out of all your sister's husbands. You will have a better life than any of them."

"And you think I care about that?"

"You should. It's well known around St. Louis that the Millers have the means. There are mothers and fathers all over the city who would love to have him for a son-in-law. You're going to have quite the life, young lady."

"But is it quite the life if it's a life I don't want?"

"How can you not want it? A husband. A nice home. Children. It's all you've wanted."

"No, it's all you've wanted. And it's all my sisters have wanted."

"Oh, spare me talk of your dreams of adventure." She rolled her eyes again and wiggled her finger at her daughter. "There is plenty of adventure in being married and having children. Trust me."

"That's not the kind of adventure I want, Mother."

"It doesn't matter what you want, Abby. Your purpose in life and in this family is to marry and have children. If you're lucky, which it looks like you are, you will marry a nice man with means. You should be happy. You could have ended up like Mirabel Pickens." Mother brushed her fingers across her forehead. "Lord only knows what her parents were thinking marrying her off to that horrible Mr. Stansbury on the edge of town. He's at least twice her age and hasn't two pennies to rub together. Of course, he acts like he does, but honestly, I think the Pickens family gives them money." Mother fanned her face with her hand. "Now, go upstairs and change your dress. Fix your hair too. He'll be here within the hour."

Before Abby could protest any further, her mother spun on her heel and marched back across the porch and into the back door of the kitchen. Abby stood on the porch. Part of her was too stunned for words, yet the other part wasn't shocked at all. She always knew this day was coming. It just had come a little sooner than she thought it would, and although she had thought of a few excuses or reasons she could give to put it off, with

Herbert on his way to the house, she didn't know if any of them would work.

Scratch that.

She knew none of them would work.

Her parents had their eyes set on the young Mr. Miller for a while, and there wasn't any reasoning they would listen to that would change their minds.

It wasn't that Herbert—or Hewy as he once told her she could call him—was a dreadful young man. He wasn't exactly what she would call the type of man she would hope to marry, but he was nice. He was taller than most men his age and skinner, and he wore thick glasses that always seemed to slip down his nose as he talked. He was constantly pushing them back up, and there were times Abby wondered if he ever would buy a pair that fit better or if he enjoyed the fact they were a size too big. Like had it become a habit for him and one he liked.

She remembered how distracting it had been at the Christmas dance last December that her parent's friends hosted at their house. Every few steps, he would take his hand off her waist to push them back up his nose, and he would even miss a step here and there, throwing them both off balance because he had to lead. He'd even stepped on her foot once or twice.

Her toe throbbed for days after that party.

No. She simply could not marry him. She just couldn't.

If her mother wouldn't see reason, perhaps her pa would.

She marched across the porch and into the house, making her way toward his office and knocking on the door.

"Come in," her pa said from the other side, and as she opened it and moved into the room, he glanced up from his desk and smiled. "Good afternoon, Abby."

"Well, it's an afternoon, but I'm not sure it's a good one."

He cocked one eyebrow and threw the pencil in his hand down onto a stack of papers on the desk. "What has your mother done now?"

"She's informed me that Mr. Herbert Miller is on his way to the house to finalize an agreement for my hand in marriage." She paused for a moment but then continued before her father could say a word. "Father, I know you aren't going to accept it. Right?"

"And what makes you say that?" He glanced down at the papers on his desk as he blew out a breath.

She knew where this conversation was headed. She'd seen this reaction in him she didn't know how many times in her life. When faced with a question that Pa didn't want to answer, he used work as his excuse to ask whoever was asking him what he didn't want to face to leave. She wasn't about to let him do it today.

"I don't care what you have on that desk that is so important, Pa, but quite frankly, I don't care. This is important. This is my future. I don't want to marry Herbert Miller. I don't love him. You've got to put a stop to this."

He reached up and rubbed his fingers into his temples. "What is it that you want me to say, Abby? I don't have time for this."

"I want you to say no and tell him that I'm not ready to marry and that you don't give him your blessing."

"You know I can't say that, young lady."

"For heaven's sakes, why not?"

"Because we've already agreed, and he's already paid off our debts."

"He's done what?" She didn't mean to shout, but she did anyway, and the look on her father's face as the loudness in her tone blared in his ears told her she should have given a second thought before letting her volume raise.

"Don't take that tone with me, young lady."

"I'm sorry, Pa. I didn't mean to. It's just that . . . I don't want to marry Herbert Miller."

"And I don't understand why you don't. He comes from a

good family—"

"And he wants to provide me with a good life. I know." She threw her hands up in the air and paced in front of her father's desk. "Mother already told me all those things. But they don't matter. It doesn't matter how good his family is or what he wants to provide for me. I don't want to be like my sisters. You know this. You've always known this."

"Don't tell me you still have all those silly notions of adventure stuck in your head."

"They aren't silly."

"But they are!" He slapped his hand down on his desk. The force was so great that it rattled the oil lamp sitting on the edge, and the flame flickered. Abby flinched, and she stared at her pa, blinking.

Of course, she'd seen her father angry a time or two growing up. She didn't think there was a child alive who didn't see their parents in a fit at least once. It was what adults did.

But while she knew he could get that angry, she didn't expect to see it. At least not today. Not over this.

He fetched an envelope, opened it, and yanked out the money tucked inside. He threw it down on the table. "Do you see this? This is what will save this family. You are what will save this family. Abby, it's time you grow up and stop wasting your time and thoughts on silly things. You're not a child anymore. You're a woman. It's time for you to marry and take care of a husband and children. I know you have never talked about wanting those things, but I thought perhaps the older you became . . ."

"Well, you thought wrong." She folded her arms across her chest.

"Perhaps I did. But that doesn't change the fact that we will make the wedding plans when this young man comes over this afternoon."

"Pa, please, no. Don't make me do this."

He held up his hands. "I'm sorry, Abby, but I've already made my decision, and the deal is done. It's what I had to do to save this house and my family. And it was the best thing I could have done for you." He moved to the office door, opening it before he paused in the frame. "Now, if you'll excuse me, I must see to the rest of my work before this young man arrives."

"Pa?"

"Abby, this conversation is finished."

Tears welled in her eyes, and although she tried to blink them away, she couldn't, and they soon found themselves spilling over and streaming down her cheeks. She shook her head as she watched him leave the office. While she knew there had been a chance he wouldn't listen to her, she hoped he might.

And now that hope was gone, leaving her with only a sense of desperation.

What could she do? She couldn't marry Herbert. She just couldn't. She would rather run away than marry him.

Run away.

That was what she would do.

That was the answer.

If she wanted adventure when no one would give it to her, well then, she would simply take it for herself.

All she needed was to pack some clothes and get her hands on some money.

Money.

She glanced over her shoulder toward the pile of cash Pa had yanked out of the envelope. She didn't know how much was there, but it looked enough. Or she should say it looked like enough to get her where she wanted to go. It was hers after all, wasn't it? If she was the one sold like a farm animal?

She moved over to the desk, staring down at the paper bills.

She didn't have to take it all. She could leave some of it for her parents.

Never mind, she thought. *I'm taking every last dollar.*

TWO

WILLIAM

*W*illiam's eyes fluttered with the booming voice that filtered into the barn from the stalls and walkway below. He rolled over, and several stalks of hay poked his back through his shirt. He hated sleeping in the hayloft of a barn, but it was safer than sleeping in a stall. Not only could a horse step on him, or worse, lay down on him in a stall, but there was a better chance he would get caught if he was down there instead of up in the hayloft.

And he couldn't get caught.

Not unless he wanted to go to jail.

Which he didn't.

"Yeah. Just take the last stall on the left, Mr. Russell. Are you boarding for the day?" another voice asked.

"I'll be back for him around dawn. That's when we leave to take another trip to Oregon. I gots me a pocket full of money, and I want to have fun spending it."

William's ears perked up with the word money, and he rolled over again, scooting on his stomach toward the edge of the loft so he could look down upon the man. He couldn't glimpse the man's face looking down on the top of his hat, but the man was dressed in all black from his hat to his chaps. He watched as the man led his buckskin horse down the walkway into the stall and untacked it before throwing the saddle on the rack and hooking the bridle on the horn. He fed and watered the animal, then strode back toward the door. The rowels of his spurs clanked and rattled with each of his steps.

William knew he needed to get out of the barn before the stable master found him. He didn't know the price he would have to pay if caught sleeping in the hayloft, but he wasn't about to find out. He rolled up onto his knees, folding his blanket before shoving it in his bag and brushing the last crumbs of the stale loaf of bread he had for dinner, so they scattered in the hay.

Looking over the edge of the loft, he glanced around, and after making sure no one would see him, he scaled down the ladder, jumping off the last rung before he slung his bag over his shoulder and darted out the back door of the barn.

~

*W*illiam hadn't ever been to Independence, Missouri before. He'd only heard about it in his brother's stories. They used to talk about coming here as young boys when they dreamed. It was known as the Queen City of the Trails. The starting point where those seeking to travel out west to the frontier started their journey. He hadn't known what to expect from this strange little city, but such didn't matter. All that did was that somehow, he found his way out of it.

And preferably by wagon on a wagon train headed to Oregon or California.

He wasn't picky about where he would go. He just needed to get as far away from Missouri as possible and by any means he could.

Even if he had to work for it.

He trotted down the different alleyways between the buildings, staying off the main streets as he veered through town. He rounded the corner onto another street, and as he did, he came face to face with a small café. Scents of eggs, bacon, sausage, and potatoes wafted in the air, and his stomach growled as though to tell him it wanted everything the nose could smell. His mouth watered too, and he closed his eyes, imagining how it all tasted—which he was sure was delicious.

He hadn't eaten anything since finding that loaf of old bread in the garbage outside of the bakery yesterday morning, and while he had planned to go back there to check for more, the thought of stale, butterless bread was no match for the smell of a hot breakfast.

Opening his eyes, he glanced down at the ground. He didn't want more stale bread any more than he wanted to dig out his own eyes, but of course, there was one big problem. How to get it? Getting the bread was easy, but with empty pockets and not a nickel to his name, the hot breakfast was nothing short of impossible.

He heaved a deep sigh and hunched his shoulders as he kicked at a rock and watched it roll several inches. Admitting defeat was never easy, and this morning with a grumbling stomach was no exception.

Still, facts were facts. He didn't have the money, so bread it was.

He continued down the street, barely looking up as he passed the café. He didn't want to see the food any more than he wanted to smell it, but as he passed, he glanced out of the corner of his eye. A young couple was sitting at a table outside, chatting to one another. Distracted with their conversation, they didn't even look at William as he passed. Hesitation spurred through him, and he slowed down, watching as the man scooted his chair toward the woman, and they huddled their faces close to one another.

"And so, I told him, Mr. Dexter, I just can't marry your daughter because I'm in love with someone else," the man said.

"Oh, and just who might that be?" the woman asked.

The man scooted his chair even closer and grabbed her hands. "Why, you, my darling." While the woman ducked her chin, her face turned a bright shade of red, and she removed her handkerchief from her handbag, brushing her other hand along her chest. William wanted to retch at the sight of their love and affection for one another, but with an empty stomach, nothing would have come up. Not to mention, he would have drawn unwanted attention from what he was about to do.

He just needed to wait for the perfect moment . . .

Just as he had hoped, the man, so overcome with love, shoved his plate aside and out of his way. William lunged over the small fence separating the dining area from the sidewalk and grabbed the plate. The woman screamed, but as the man spun in his chair, William took off down the street with the plate tucked tight into his body so none of the food would spill.

⁓

*W*illiam continued down the street and around another building, hiding behind several wooden crates stacked against the brick wall. He pressed his back against the bricks and glanced down both directions of the alleyway before sliding down to the ground and tucking his legs up until he was blocked from sight.

His lungs heaved, and he closed his eyes. "Lord. Please forgive me for stealing this food. I know it's wrong, and I have sinned. I hate to eat it, but . . . I'm starving. I pray for my forgiveness. In Jesus' name. Amen."

Although the first bite tasted like a little bit of heaven, the guilt gave it an unpleasant aftertaste. It was one he didn't like, but he also knew that he didn't know when he would see food again without stealing. He wanted to curse himself just as much as he wanted to curse his brother for putting him into this mess. And yet, he also knew that doing either of those wouldn't make the situation better.

Nothing would make it better.

Well, clearing his name would.

But knowing the solution and putting it into play were two different things. Pinkertons weren't about hearing reason. They just saw the words as excuses. The guilty are always trying to get out of punishment for their crimes, they would say, and no matter what he told them, they would only say it to him.

They wouldn't believe him.

Nor would they even give him the chance to explain.

He shoveled the last few bites of eggs into his mouth, both wanting to chew them slowly to savor them and also gobble them down so he could flee before anyone caught him. Once he had licked it clean, he tossed the plate aside, and another hint of guilt prickled in his chest as the bone white china smacked against the dirt with a thud sound. He wanted to return the plate to the café, and yet he knew that it would be foolish to do so.

Perhaps I can leave it outside the door tonight after dark, he thought. Do at least one good thing today, even if it's not much of one.

It would be the right thing to do.

He could almost hear his mama talking to him from Heaven above, telling him what he needed to do. Or course, that was nothing new. He listened to her daily, always on his case about one thing or another he did. Lord, she would roll over in her grave if she saw him now. He was glad she passed on so she wouldn't have to see the utter failure he'd become. As much as he hated to think that, he did, and it was just another thing to hate his brother for.

He heaved a deep sigh and slipped his hand into his pants pocket, pulling out a folded piece of paper. It was yellower than it had been months ago, and the edges were tearing from all the time spent in his pocket, and all the times he pulled it out, looked at it, and stuck it back in. It wasn't that looking at it gave him hope or comfort. It was just the opposite, actually. The paper only brought him fear, pain, and anger, and although he wanted to throw it away every second of every day, he also wanted to keep it. He didn't know why.

Perhaps it was the reminder he needed.

Or perhaps he was nothing but an utter fool.

He didn't know which.

But as he opened it and looked down upon the words 'WANTED' and a drawn picture of his face with his name below written in black ink, all the feelings came flooding back.

He was a wanted man.

And it was all his brother's fault.

ORDER OR READ FOR FREE WITH KINDLE UNLIMITED

To my sister
Michelle Renee Horning

April 3, 1973 - January 8, 2022
You will be forever missed. I don't know how I will do this thing called
life without you.

London James is a pen name for Angela Christina Archer. She lives on a ranch with her husband, two daughters, and many farm animals. She was born and raised in Nevada and grew up riding and showing horses. While she doesn't show anymore, she still loves to trail ride.

From a young age, she always wanted to write a novel. However, every time the desire flickered, she shoved the thought from my mind until one morning in 2009, she awoke with the determination to follow her dream.

WWW.AUTHORLONDONJAMES.COM

Join my mailing list for news on releases, discounted sales, and exclusive member-only benefits!

28867346R00099